A Christmas
Carol for Candy

PEGGY URRY

Give kindness

♡ *Peggy Urry*

Other works in this collection:

Christmas Future by Valerie Ipson
Eleanor and the Christmas Carol Fudge by Tamara Passey

This is a work of fiction. The names, characters, and incidents are the product of the author's fabulous imagination. Any resemblance to actual persons living or dead, business establishments, events, locales, or your imagination is entirely coincidental.

Cover: McKenna Lee, Sage Fox Design

Although this copy has editing errors, I hope you enjoy it. A ected copy is available on Amazon.

If you do enjoy the story, please consider leaving a review on zon and Goodreads.

Keep up-to-date with projects I am working on by following me:

| Facebook | Instagram | Blog | Amazon |

Chapter 1

Candy Kaine's fingers tightened around the steering wheel. She wanted to be back home already, checking on Edie before settling in to finish her homework. She hoped Molly wouldn't interrupt as she frequently did with her need for some pantry item. But first, she had to traverse the mountain pass amid the late afternoon travelers.

Shepherd's Pass--the easiest way into Saint Angelo--had a light covering of snow, but nothing too ominous. Yet. The weather here was always unpredictable. She took the road as quickly as she dared. Snow had fallen intermittently in the city throughout the day. At the crest of the first hill, it turned to sleet. Nothing had stuck to the roads, but people still drove as if it had.

Candy's fingers tapped the wheel impatiently as she passed a slowing van. They probably had people to help with their to-do lists. Not her. She didn't need that. What she *did* need was for everyone to move over so she didn't have to weave in and out of traffic. Edie would be worried when she didn't show up on time, even if she called. Thursday classes had ended early, but this puttering traffic had landed her ten minutes behind schedule.

Coming down the pass into Saint Angelo, warning signs for the near-hairpin curve known as Shepherd's Hook stood sentinel on the roadside. Only a fool would disregard them. She applied the brakes, easing her car around the bend. The twinkling lights of Saint Angelo appeared in the distance, glittering in the deepening dusk. The small town sprawled a few miles below, curving around the lake and running along the mountain bench. It was like the suns she had drawn as a child, dense in the center with straggling rays leaking

1

outward—a sun that had elongated and fallen over on its side.

Candy had moved here for two reasons: to escape her family's censure and take advantage of the cheap rent. The criticism might have been palatable if it had involved things like a messy room (although hers never was) or a life plan (which she had), but it didn't; it was over her philandering fiancé. So, when Aunt Zathra had offered a rental property in Saint Angelo, Candy had snatched it up like hot cocoa at the ski lodge.

The quaint town was just what she'd needed and she'd immersed herself in work and school with some home-care clients providing income on the side. School and work filled her days and every bit of her heart. They left no time for relationships. They allowed no consideration of her stepmother's biting words about her broken engagement or her father's opinion that she was throwing away her only chance at marriage. Like she was spinster at age twenty-two.

As if Andrew had been doing her a favor. Ugh. He was as fake as her father's toupee and not half as nice. It had surprised her that the remorse she felt was not over the break-up, it was over not having done it sooner.

After that dreadful scene at the rehearsal and Andrew's childish tantrum, she had cut off all communication with him. No more critical comments about her off-brand clothes or her tardiness. She had purged her life of everything that reminded her of him. He refused to accept that she was serious about ending things and continued contacting her. Finally, she blocked him on her phone, all her social media, and her e-mail.

Why was she even thinking about all that drama tonight? It probably had to do with all those engagement advertisements on the radio recently. Even as she laid blame, another jewelry store ad started. It was a stark reminder of last Christmas season's debacle. She flipped off the radio. She would have to find time to make some new playlists. She'd deleted the ones from before the break-up. They had all been lies anyway, especially those lists she'd created of 'their' songs.

The Saint Angelo exit approached as the car's clock changed to 5:25. It would still take another fifteen minutes to get home and over to her neighbor Mrs. Marlowe's, or Edie as she insisted on being called. She was Candy's newest client and scheduled for the end of the day, since she lived just next door. Candy had driven like a bat out of you-know-where for nothing. Picking up the phone, she instructed it to call Edie.

"Candy, dear? Is that you?" Edie's voice was full of concern.

"Yes, Edie. I'm so sorry, but I'm running behind. It's been snowing a bit today, and there were, you know, a bunch of slow drivers over the pass."

"Are you almost home?"

Candy hated the tightness in Edie's voice.

"Just getting off the highway."

"Oh, good. I was starting to worry. The weather can take a wild turn over that pass."

"Nothing is sticking yet," Candy assured her. "I should be there in about fifteen minutes."

"That will be perfect, dear. The clam chowder should be done by then. You know it was my Henry's favorite."

"Edie! You're supposed to be taking it easy," Candy chided.

"Oh, it's nothing. Just a bit of cooking. Besides, I wasn't up much."

"Mm. I'm sure." Edie chuckled softly at her comment.

3

"At least relax now. I'll be there soon."

They hung up and a few minutes later, Candy pulled into a bakery on the edge of town. Their biscuits were fluffy layers of melt-in-your-mouth buttery goodness and would be a perfect match for Edie's clam chowder. She broke off a little piece of one as she got in the car. Fresh from the oven, the delicious blend of flavors dissolved on her tongue. It was a bread-lover's dream. An epicurean delight. She closed her eyes and sank into her seat, savoring the last bit before pulling out of the parking lot. Andrew had forbidden the eating of anything resembling bread. He feared she would out-grow her wedding dress. Not that she had to think about that now. She pushed the thoughts away and drove straight home.

With her SUV parked in her garage, she walked next door to Edie's house. She knocked as she walked in. Edie sat on the couch, watching TV.

"I brought a surprise," Candy said with a grin.

Edie clapped once, "Oh what did you bring?"

"Biscuits to go with the chowder."

Edie's eyes got big and then her brow furrowed. "How did you have time to make them?"

"Oh, I didn't. You won't want my biscuits after you taste these. Loads of butter, I'm sure."

Edie started to stand.

"Don't get up, I'll make you a tray."

"That would be nice, dear. You know, my Jace makes the best cast iron skillet biscuits."

"Does he now?"

Jace apparently had a never-ending list of things he did 'best'. She didn't begrudge him that one bit. Well, maybe she did a half a bit. It would be nice to have someone think you were the best at something.

4

Edie merely nodded in response, then added, "And he's quite handsome too. Like his dad."

"Are you sure?" Candy teased making her way to the kitchen. She tapped the ski photo on the fridge as she passed it. "I think this photo has been doctored up somehow," she called to the living room.

One of the four teenage boys was Jace, but she had no idea which one. They all stood, helmets tucked under an arm, posing with their snowboards. The boys wore colorful ski pants and coats, smiling as brightly as the wintry slopes they were standing on. The photo was held in place by an SAHS Ski Team magnet.

"Or maybe it's a picture from a magazine."

"Now you're teasing me. Those are all good boys."

"Of course they are; they had you spoiling them," Candy said.

Grinning, she turned back to the photo. As always, her eye went straight to the boy in the sapphire blue jacket. She would have crushed on him so hard back in high school. Secretly, of course. Doodling his initials with swirls and hearts on the back of her notebooks to pass time during History class.

Edie had never clarified which was her grandson but there was no way Mr. Perfect could also be the hottest guy in the picture. He would be the goofy-looking one on the end. It was hard to tell. Edie said Jace looked like his dad, but the family photos on the mantle were small and made discerning what Jace might look like difficult. The larger ones hanging down the hall had been taken when the grandchildren were young. Not that it mattered. According to Edie, he hadn't come back to Saint Angelo since he went off to college.

Today, rather than give the photo a passing glance, she lingered and actually took in the details of the photo. The date printed at the bottom was eight years ago. She imagined the boy turned man, a little scruffy, a little broader through the shoulders. Her heart sighed. He would be unfairly handsome now. And would, of course, be happily married and have a couple of beautiful children. She pushed all those thoughts, plus the longing that they invoked, out of her mind. Her schedule was too full for that anyway.

When Candy lifted the lid from the soup pot, steam swirled up from the chowder. The comforting, down-home smells of cream, clams, and potatoes wafted into the kitchen. Her mouth watered in anticipation. This was definitely good for the soul. After filling the bowls, she loaded little ramekins with butter and Edie's homemade jam and set them on plates with the biscuits. Contentment settled around her as she delivered one of the trays to the end table near Edie.

"Are you going to sit with me tonight?" Edie asked muting the commercial

"For a bit, but I've got loads of homework, some laundry, and a project to do."

Edie paused with the spoon halfway to her mouth. "You work too hard. You need to get out and have some fun. And wear something besides yoga pants all the time."

Candy fumbled for a response. "These are scrubs, not yoga pants. And fun? That was, um, surprising you with these biscuits," she said. "Besides, you know I have to keep my grades up."

"I know—that scholarship is your life." Edie frowned as she said it.

"It pays for school, Edie."

"But it's making you forget to live."

"No, it isn't."

She clearly was living. Sitting right here in Edie's living room eating savory clam chowder. Edie cocked her head;

apparently, she disagreed. Not wanting to discuss it anymore, Candy stared into her clam chowder, stirring it to let the heat escape. Edie didn't say anything more, but went back to watching TV.

A commercial for the Hallmark channel advertised the weekly line-up. They'd been promoting their season premieres for well over a month. Candy did her best to avoid them, which was one of reasons she rarely stayed long at Edie's. True to form, Edie clicked the channel to the Hallmark station.

They didn't mind deceiving viewers by showing how lovely a Christmas romance was. Well it wasn't lovely. Not when your boyfriend proposed in front of your whole family at the Annual Christmas Gala after he'd just had a tryst with your step-mom and blamed you. Not when your fiancé chose to continue his philandering and your best friend/coworker/Maid of Honor chose to oblige. Why was she even thinking of him again? Stupid Christmas romances.

She stirred her soup again, no longer wanting to eat.

"I'm sorry if I upset you, dear."

Sipping a tiny bit from her spoon to avoid more questions from Edie, Candy rolled the warm flavors over her tongue.

"You didn't," said Candy as she gathered the bowls.

"You've hardly eaten." Edie's voice wavered with concern.

"I have a big test tomorrow." Candy was anxious to review her notes in the quiet of her own home.

"Have you started finals already? It's still November."

"No, not finals, just the last test before the final." Candy headed to the kitchen. "I'll finish eating while I clean up in here."

It wasn't long before she reached for her coat and purse.

"Good luck on your test," said Edie. "I'm sure you'll do

7

just fine."

Several hours later the words on the page swam together. She rubbed her eyes and checked the clock. More than three hours had passed. Taking a short break, she folded her last load of laundry and began a short stretching routine.

Her mind wandered back to Andrew. He'd seemed so interested at first, supportive of her goals. But he'd encouraged her to work more and go to school less so they could save for a house. Then, it was all work and no school.

She'd been grateful he hadn't pressured her too often to be intimate. It was only after their engagement that she realized he, personally, had no intention of saving such closeness for marriage. But she lacked the courage to walk away. Surely he wouldn't do that once they were married.

The memories still caused pain, stemming mostly from humiliation. She let them wash over her.

On the night of the wedding rehearsal, she had arrived at the church so early not even the wedding party had been there. She had hoped to calm her nerves but the opposite happened. The tension exploded into a breath-stealing panic attack. Ducking into the nearest classroom to pull herself together, she clutched her stomach where her heart had dropped. Bending slightly she tried to slow her breathing and the dread rushing through her veins. Minutes passed. Rather than peace, voices floated on the air, coming closer, escalating her alarm. No one could see her like this. No one.

Her eyes, now adjusted to the darkened room, darted around in search of a place to hide. The rolling bookcase in the corner would have to do. Pushing it away from the wall, she dropped behind it just as the door opened.

The groom, followed by the giggling Maid of Honor, tumbled inside, oblivious to anything but each other. The air around Candy tightened and she found herself paralyzed.

Her eyelids refused to close, to block the scene. This was not happening. Except it was. Steeling her nerves, she drew in a silent, slow breath, closed her eyes and covered her ears with her fists. Her newly-manicured nails dug into her palms, the physical pain vying against the emotional for center stage.

A knock on the door yanked her from Memory Lane. Molly, from across the street, walked in.

"Hey Candy, what're you up to?"

"Studying for a test tomorrow." *And replaying a nightmare.*

"Oh. I don't want to interrupt, but do you care if I hang out for a bit?"

Candy's mouth dropped. No request for an egg or cup of sugar? Pulling herself together she motioned to the couch and said, "I can only talk for a minute though because I've still got a few pages to study."

"That's fine, I was actually looking for some peace and quiet." She sighed as she settled into the sofa. "I told Ty I had to have a break, but where do you go this late in a town that shuts down at eight o'clock at night?"

Molly leaned back and closed her eyes. This was a change. Candy knew she should study, but her concern for Molly won.

"The girls were a little crazy today, I take it."

Molly opened one eye then shut it again.

"Who knew that a four year old could lead a six year old into so much trouble? Usually Gracie runs the show, but not today." She put an arm over her face. "Ty is amazing with them, though, so he's going to text me when they're asleep." After another deep breath she said, "Thanks for lending me a couch." Then with a laugh she said, "I promise not to take it home."

Another hour ticked by before Ty texted Molly the all clear. Once she left, Candy massaged her temples as she studied the last of the bullet points on her study sheet. She was ready. Well, as ready as she was going to be. She would go through it once more in the morning just in case.

Chapter 2

Pacing the kitchen where a table should be, Jace Marlowe rubbed his hands for warmth. *Think, Jace, think.* He looked around the mostly bare apartment. There was nothing left to sell. The expensive paintings were gone, as was the handcrafted leather furniture. Even the giant sheepskin rug, crystal chandelier and silk floor pillows were all gone. The only things left were his computer—which he needed for work—and the coffee table he'd already put in the ads. It was nearly December and so far, no one was interested in ridiculously expensive furniture, even at a fraction of its cost.

Resentment welled inside him. If only he'd seen past the pretty face and false promises to Liz's character. He'd seen it once when a co-worker crossed her, but he'd thought it had been an isolated incident. Come to find out, no one crossed her and survived.

Guess what, Lizzy? I will survive.

The kitchen counter had become his desk. A wooden stool, rescued from the apartment complex's trash bin, served as his only chair. Jace stopped pacing in front of the computer. The web page mock-up he'd finished for Raxoco Resorts and Spas was ready. The question now was whether they would look past the myriad false reviews Liz and company had left and give him a chance to show them what he could do.

He'd worked on it most of the day and it looked good. Clean lines, rich earth tones, and easy navigation menus blended function and style in a way he thought reflected Raxoco's aesthetic. Another scan of the page resulted in a minor adjustment to the layout and some of the text. It wasn't perfect, but he figured they would want to change

11

some things anyway.

He blew air onto his cold fingers. What he'd give for a cup of hot coffee, warming his fingers with the mug, breathing the smell of early morning, watching the steam rise as he waited for it to cool enough to drink. But it wasn't morning and it wouldn't be today.

Today was the end of the week, the end of the month. He rubbed the two-day growth on his face. Maybe it was also the end of his career. He sent up a half-hearted prayer asking one more time for a break. Luck hadn't been too kind lately, so he didn't expect any concessions, but he hadn't given up on hope either.

The phone buzzed and after a glance at the Caller ID, he felt his heart sink in disappointment. Grandma Edie. He paused, contemplating whether to let it go to voicemail. Raxoco would likely ring in the middle of his grandma's call. But guilt won over. He'd make it short, though.

"Hello, Grandma."

They exchanged their usual greetings and lies about life being fine. He glanced at his phone. There were no other calls coming in, but he didn't want to risk it.

"I've got an appointment soon, so I can't talk long today, " he said.

"No problem dear, I know how busy you and Kat are. I just wondered if you were coming out for Christmas this year. I won't be able to drive until after New Year's so I'm trying to make some plans."

And I'm trying to keep a roof over my head.

" I don't know about Kat, I haven't talked to her about it. But I've got a couple of big designs I'm working on right now so I don't think I'll be able to make it."

He had no idea what his sister's plans were, but for him, there was no reason to go back. Nothing in St. A appealed to him. Except maybe the ski slopes. Best skiing there was, but he hadn't even been back for that.

Before he could change the subject, she said, "Someday you're going to have to face your demons."

Seemed Grandma Edie was in a mood today. With no desire to go down that road he said, "Maybe next year, then. How's your foot?"

"It's fine dear. Miss Peddle to the Metal next door checks in on me."

Oh, she really was in a mood. Usually the girl next door was nothing short of perfect.

"She's endangered you with her driving?" He teased in an effort to cheer her up.

"No." His grandma huffed and he imagined the eye roll that probably went with it. "She just goes through life too fast. In and out of here in five minutes lately. But she's always very sweet, so I really shouldn't complain."

That concerned Jace. "How does she check on you in five minutes? Is that enough time?"

"That is a bit of an exaggeration. She usually whips up dinner and gobbles it down so she can run home. So busy all the time. I think I'm one of her projects she's always working on."

He'd probably been Liz's project.

Grandma Edie interrupted his thoughts, " I really worry about her. How do you kids say it these days? Life in the fast lane, living large, lit?"

Aside from the 'lit' part, it definitely sounded like his ex but he chuckled at his grandma's expressions.

"There's not much of a fast lane in St. A."

"Oh, you'd be surprised, dear. Mrs. Tarrington claims she is going all out this year to win the 'Holiday Spirit' award at the Town Fair."

The town tradition consisted of holiday activities beginning with a menorah lighting to start Hanukkah and ending New Year's Eve with the Town Fair.

He suppressed a smile. "Sounds daring."

Grandma Edie let out something between a grunt and a cough. Either way, it was full of disgust. "Well you know who won't be in the running? Your grandmother." That knife landed squarely in his gut. "Because no one is here to help me get the decorations up." Twist. "But no matter …" The false cheeriness drove the knife deeper. "I'll see you at family dinner in a few months when I can drive again."

"Sure thing." He wanted to say he'd come back, that together, they would out-do Mrs. Tarrington, but the past was too big of a monster. The least he could do was lighten things up. "But you'll be singing in the Christmas Concert right?"

"Christmas Chorale, and yes. My usual part."

"There you go, that Christmas spirit right there will outdo anything Mrs. Tarrington can produce."

"You're just trying to placate me."

"Not true. I know it's been a while since I heard the Chorale, but your part was always my favorite."

"You're a dear. It's hard for me that you've all grown up and moved away. I always wish for my family to be there, but at least we still have our first-Sunday dinners." The mood had returned with an edge of melancholy. "Which I will miss this week, but no matter." Then under her breath she said, "Darn foot."

"Make sure Speed Demon takes good care of it for you."

"Well, she'll be by in a little while. I whipped up some clam chowder last night and she stayed a bit, so maybe she'll stay again."

The chowder sounded divine and his stomach grumbled in

agreement. Maybe he should make a trip over the mountain today. But then the storm would hit and he would be stuck there until the roads were cleared.

Hoping to cheer her up he said, "No one makes chowder like you do."

Grandma Edie tsk-ed at his comment and said, "It's never the same without your biscuits. Even the ones she brought from the bakery don't rival yours."

"Mine would probably ruin it." He laughed. "I haven't made biscuits since high school."

"We might be having them again tonight. She insisted on making dinner, but it will probably be burgers from the drive-thru. At least if she made dinner I'd have company."

Jace hated the wistfulness in her voice.

"It's Friday, so maybe she will have more time tonight."

"I hope so, but she's always running off somewhere. She's busy like I know you are, so I'll get back to my show and waiting."

She'd emphasized 'busy' and 'waiting'. A pang went through Jace. But he needed this job, so he said goodbye.

Chapter 3

Rising early, Candy twisted her hair into a messy bun, showered, and threw on a spot of makeup. Nibbling a protein bar she reviewed her notes for an hour. A glance at the clock confirmed that she only had a few minutes before she would need to leave for the testing center at Mack Community College, which opened at 8:00 a.m. It was enough for a quick check of the weather and e-mail.

The weather predicted another overcast, dreary day. It should have predicted turbulent storms.

No messages were in her inbox, but one new message waited for her in the Spam folder: the message from her ex that she'd expected, and dreaded, for nine months. Anxiety squeezed her chest like a vice. It was like the phone call in the middle of the night that you don't want to answer it because it could only be bad news, yet you have to pick up.

Nine months of silence had eased Candy into a tenuous comfort. In a split second it caved under the weight of memories. She gripped the counter and closed her eyes as if it would somehow make the message disappear. Laying her head on the cool counter, she took a deep breath. And another. Months ago, she would have deleted it without hesitation and chanced suffering weeks of guilt afterward.

Perhaps the holiday season, where kindness and cheer permeated the atmosphere, had lulled her into thinking she could deal with it. Perhaps the memory of their engagement last Christmas gave her more pause and a bit of curiosity. Or perhaps the more palatable of her choices was circumventing the guilt. It didn't really matter which one she chose. They all led to the same thing. One small click and her world tilted.

Hey, babe!

I can't seem to get you off my mind lately. I miss running my fingers through your silky hair. We need to reconnect and the holidays are a perfect time for that. I'm willing to give us another chance and I can't help thinking if you hadn't been such a nun, I wouldn't have had to turn to other women. We were so good together. We absolutely deserve another chance. It's time to get off the shelf and join the real world. I'll be in Saint Angelo in a few weeks on business. I'll let you know when I can meet you for dinner and some fun.

Andrew

P.S. I have some good news about the fund.

She stared at the unsolicited message that taunted her from the laptop's screen. The anger was gone and that scared her. When she had let go of the anger, she had also let go of her defense against his attacks. She took a deep breath. *Calm and cool.* She could do this. But the words shattered the quiet peace of her rental house, invaded her space, and made her feel small again.

No. She wouldn't give him that kind of control over her. It didn't matter that he had tracked her to Saint Angelo, that he wanted to meet for dinner and *fun.* Not happening. No way would she get pulled into that circus again, where she always felt like the clown, juggling the ringmaster's lies and indiscretions.

And the fund? The only good news there would be that he'd somehow managed to get her 'investment' back. That would be helpful—and maybe a reason to meet him. Since leaving her family in the city, she'd barely made ends meet.

Another e-mail arrived from Andrew.

17

Candice.

He always called her that with thinned lips and narrowed eyes. A critical lecture invariably followed.

Unfortunately, there are few upscale restaurants to choose from, so you'll just have to put aside your distaste for seafood. I'll pick you up Monday the 17th at 6:00 sharp and I mean sharp, so for once, don't make me wait.
Andrew

It took three tries to type the simple response. *No.* Then she blocked his e-mail. Again. Her heart pounded. She closed her eyes and took a deep breath.

When she finally checked the clock, she nearly choked. How did time move so quickly?

Grabbing her backpack and keys, she raced out the door, juggling the bag and her coat as she shoved her arms into it. If she didn't hurry, she would have to blow through the Psych 3 test in order to pick up her Friday care-giving client on time.

Mr. Lewiston was very meticulous. The small details mattered to him. He reminded Candy of her late grandfather, whom she'd adored so much that he got a pass when it came to his strictness.

Candy knew better than to race through town on snow-covered streets, but she still pushed it. The Cherokee continued to surprise her with its easy handling of bad weather conditions. She pulled into the parking lot with a bit of drift around the corner and chose the closest spot to the entrance. By the looks of the parking lot, only a few students were here today.

Dread overcame her need to rush. She sat in her car,

defying the ticking clock. One minute, she would give herself one minute. She took quick, shallow breaths as she tapped the steering wheel with apprehension as the heater blazed against the frigid temperatures outside. Nothing eased the trepidation building inside her.

Festive decorations sparkled around the exterior of the old Janssen manor that Mack Community College used as a satellite campus and testing center. Large wreaths decorated in silver and blue ribbons hung from the front two windows on the ground floor. Menorahs sat in the sills waiting to be lit. Their attempt at cheer did nothing to penetrate the gloom that hung thick inside her car.

When she couldn't put it off any longer, she left the comfort of her car. Icy air pricked her skin as she hurried toward the building. This Psych 3 test wasn't the final, but the score would determine her future before she walked back out.

Every spare hour during the past week had been spent pouring over the textbook and her class notes. Last night, she had checked grades on the online portal in between study times. The solid 89 percent hadn't budged all semester, even with the number of hours she spent immersed in the subject. No one could predict the random questions that always ended the tests. Questions she didn't know the answer to, like, "Which teams played in Super Bowl XXX and who won?"

In order to keep her scholarship, she needed a perfect score. No tuition waiver meant searching for more gigs like selling tickets to the local Christmas Chorale. She preferred more clients who needed care-giving because those jobs lasted longer, but in such a small town, those weren't the easiest to find. More work also meant fewer classes, which pushed graduation even further away. Pulling her courage tight like her coat, she hustled toward the manor. She reached for anything to take her mind off the gloom she felt.

Stuffy air that was too warm to be comfortable greeted her. A couple of students looked up from decorating the fireplace mantle as she walked in. They quickly went back to setting up their candles and decorations of red, green, and black. She would rather learn more about Kwanza, but the test and Mr. Lewiston wouldn't wait. Maybe later.

Candy unfastened her coat and headed past the fresh-cut Christmas tree. Aside from the twinkling lights, the mascot, and school colors, it was a collection of various holiday traditions. Ornaments ranged from menorahs and dreidels to Kwanza figurines to candy canes and reindeer. The pine scent was a welcome change from the usual staleness that permeated the rooms. The door to the Testing Center was just down the hall. 'Center' probably wasn't the appropriate term. Maybe Closet? A total of four testing stations, with computers and privacy screens, occupied a small table to the right of the proctor's desk.

Ashley, a fellow student and the morning proctor, looked up. "Oh, hey, Candy," she said.

"Hey, Ash. Gotta take the Psych 3 test," Candy said while checking in.

Her attempted cheerfulness didn't alleviate the nervousness stomping around in her stomach. She gave Ashley her student number as she stowed her gear in the cubbies by the door. "Wish me luck."

"Good luck, girl. I think you're going to need it." Ashley's grimaced in sympathy. "Another student was complaining about it a few minutes ago. You probably saw him on your way out."

She shook her head. "No, I didn't see anyone." She closed her eyes for a second and took another deep breath. With a genuine smile she said, "Thanks, Ash."

She sat down and started the test. Only half the questions covered topics she'd studied. Where the others had come from she wasn't sure. On par, the teacher threw in a random question. Today's mystery: "Where does Hitler currently reside?" She was certain they hadn't covered *that* in class. It seriously bugged her. What was the point of studying the textbook and her notes when impossible questions dotted the exams? She rubbed her temples, contemplating a sassy response.

Hitler currently resides six feet under. But was there a psychological connection? She decided to expound. *Due to his antisocial personality disorder, he should be quite content alone. If not, his schizophrenic visions and fantasies of redeeming Germany will keep him company.*

The teacher would probably fail her, so she highlighted it and clicked 'next'. The final question asked her to order Maslow's hierarchy of needs from bottom to top. Basic psychology. A bonus after that last question. Physiological, Safety, Love/Belonging, Esteem, Self-Actualization. Studying the pyramid, her heart began to sink. She barely fit into the second category.

According to Maslow, unless she achieved a bit more safety in her life, love would be out of reach. Well, that was just fine. She wasn't ready for love right now. Besides, love—also known as Andrew—had proven heart-breaking and she'd left him at the church after the whole debacle with the Maid of Honor. It may have been the best and only decision she'd made in the whole course of their two years of dating.

The test score came up on screen. Eighty-nine percent. Perhaps only good enough if the professor decided to grade on a curve. That, however, was unlikely. She fell one rung lower on the safety scale as her scholarship was definitely in jeopardy.

"How'd you do?" asked Ashley.

"Decent, but not good enough for the 'A' I need," Candy said gathering her things.

"Sorry about that. I wish I had good news to make your day better, but I only have bad news."

"What do you mean?" Candy would probably be sorry she asked, but as long as she was taking lumps, why not?

"They're talking about closing this campus."

"What? No."

Candy stood speechless as Ashley nodded. "Apparently Raxoco Resorts thinks it's prime real estate for a luxury destination and wedding center."

"What? That doesn't make any sense. Who wants to come here to get married? It's just a one-horse town in the hills."

Ashley laughed. "I think we graduated from 'one-horse' a long time ago. With a lake in the summer and ski slopes in the winter, this is destined to be the next Aspen." Her eyes glazed over and a dreamy smile appeared.

"Then it will lose its small town charm as hordes of people come looking for the famous."

That wiped away the far-off look Ashley's face and she shrugged as she came back down to earth.

"It'll be good tourist business. The town could use a little extra traffic. Plus, it'll mean more jobs for us."

Although that might be good—since it appeared her future would need another job—Candy shook her head. She felt herself sliding farther down that safety ladder. With the threat of the school closing, graduation would be all the more difficult. She would be a CNA forever, taking all the worst parts of nursing because she wasn't a registered nurse.

She thanked Ashley again and left the building. Her

Friday started feeling like the uphill battle of a Monday after a nice weekend. Most of the time, she enjoyed her busiest day, but the disappointment from her test results and the information from Ashley hung around like a dark cloud.

She started her car, but sat, staring numbly out at the gray skies. Tiny flakes drifted about on the shifting air. Could it get any worse? It definitely would if she didn't get moving. Mr. Lewiston hated tardiness.

It had only taken one sharp reprimand months ago to convince her to arrive five minutes early and stay five minutes late each week. She drove as fast as she dared, thankful the snow hadn't begun to stick to the roads. The car in front of her slid to the side of the road. She slowed to see if they would be able to recover, but the car didn't move. Turning on her flashers, she pulled behind them and got out. As she did, the other driver's door swung open and a teenaged boy came out gushing curse words. His visible breath huffed in short spurts.

"Hey," Candy said.

"What d'you want?" The antagonism was obvious as he surveyed his situation.

She held up her hands in surrender and said, "Just seeing if I can help you get unstuck, that's all."

He looked at her and then her car. "Uh, I doubt it, lady."

"It really doesn't look too bad. I could push and see if that works, or I can hook my tow line to your car."

His face scrunched in anger. "I'm not on drugs, OK?"

Her mouth dropped open but nothing came out. The boy turned away, throwing his arms in the air.

"Wait," Candy said. When he looked back she continued, "I'm late for an appointment. If you want help, I'm here to get you back on the road. If not, you can wait for the police or the tow truck."

23

"Sure lady." The sarcasm remained. "Whatever you think will work," he said scowling.

"Let's give it a push then since that takes less time if it works."

Another driver pulled up behind Candy's SUV and rolled down his window.

"Need some muscle?" he yelled.

It wasn't evident whether he had any or not, but she wouldn't turn down assistance.

"Yes, that would be great."

The man jumped out and stood next to Candy at the back of the boy's car. He shouted some instructions and after a few pushes the stuck car eased onto the road.

"Thank you," the boy yelled out his window as he roared away.

After thanking the other driver, she hurried to the warmth of her car. There was nothing she could do about her poor time management skills now and since she didn't want to end up off the road, she drove cautiously.

Mr. Lewiston's driveway still had a bit of snow left over from the snowstorm a few days ago. Boot prints tracked up the sidewalk to the mailbox on the porch. She made a mental note to clear it before the Post Office complained. Mr. Lewiston opened the door before she could knock, his thick white hair meticulously combed back as usual.

"You're a bit late today, Candy."

This was actually nicer than she had anticipated. A sheepish smile popped up before she could stop it. "Better than a lot late, no?" She hoped that would get her a pass on the punctuality lecture.

He shuffled out the door, leaning on his cane while he locked up. "I suppose." Between the handrail and the cane, he stiffly managed the stairs. "But a good employee knows how to manage the clock. Besides, I've been looking forward to that short stack all week."

The lecture may be only one sentence today, but the way her morning had gone, Candy expected a torrent of wisdom to follow. To distract him she said, "And by 'short stack' you mean Miss Stacey and the extra buttermilk syrup?" She waggled her eyebrows at him.

"Humph. Not talkin' about nothin' but pancakes." He frowned and continued, "Besides, you know we're friends. We worked together on the Outreach committee at church before our spouses passed."

Candy just nodded. As much as he tried to keep it secret, Candy had seen through the guise of 'pancakes' within minutes of their first visit. Part of her sighed in relief as it seemed the chiding had been averted.

The drive to Hearth Oven Cafe lasted ten minutes. And it took less than that to be seated at their usual table near the window. Stacey almost always came right out, but today, a waitress whose nametag read 'Patsy' approached. With her gray hair pulled back in a bun, she didn't appear much younger than the sixty-something Miss Stacey. Mr. Lewiston's eyes narrowed in suspicion.

"Where's Miss Stacey?"

"She's off today, hun." She poured a coffee for Mr. Lewiston and gestured inquiringly to Candy.

"No thanks, I'll have an acai green tea, please."

"Be right back with that and to take your order."

"We're ready now," Mr. Lewiston grumped.

Candy smirked behind her menu as Mr. Lewiston ordered his short stack. "And Miss Stacey always brings me extra buttermilk syrup."

"No problem." Patsy made notes on her pad.

"I'm going to shake it up today," Candy said more to Mr.

Lewiston than to Patsy. "I'll do the Diablo omelet with house potatoes and a side of fruit." She handed the menus to the waitress. "Thanks, Patsy."

Patsy nodded and scurried off.

"Tomorrow is December 1st," Mr. Lewiston said regarding Candy.

"Yes. It is." She fingered the edge of her napkin wishing she could avoid where the conversation was going.

"The kids'll be here soon." He nodded as he spoke. "We need to get the decorations set up. Today."

Candy nodded, forcing down the lump in her throat. She loved Christmas, the music, the decorations, and the traditions. But when she had left the city in the spring, she'd left everything, her family, her friends, her job, and anything that didn't fit in the two suitcases she borrowed from Aunt Zathra. She'd ended up in Aunt Z's rental house in Saint Angelo, barely able to pay the bills, let alone buy groceries or holiday decor. Perhaps next year she could at least get a tree.

They talked more about his children and grandchildren and their Christmas plans. Candy had only one Christmas plan for this year: get through it.

Patsy brought a cup of hot water, lemons, and the usual tea infuser filled with leaves. "Your order will be up shortly," she said.

***

Mr. Lewiston paid the bill. They'd agreed that Candy was off the clock at breakfast. Her contribution was driving and his was buying.

"We should stop and get a tree from Santa's Tree Lot," Mr. Lewiston said.

"That's the opposite direction from your home, why not stop at Al's Terrific Trees?"

Mr. Lewiston stared out the window and took a moment before answering. "Because I like Santa more than Al."

What? Are we in third grade again?

"Santa can be kind of creepy." She steered the car out of the parking lot as she continued, "I mean, the guy sneaks into people's homes, he watches when you're sleeping, he ..."

Mr. Lewiston held up his wrinkled hand. "True, but maybe Al does that too. Now who's creepy?"

Candy burst out laughing. "I'll be sure to lock my doors and windows, just in case." She shook her head. "Poor Al probably can't compete with Santa's Tree Lot."

When they arrived at the tree lot, Mr. Lewiston promptly flagged down a worker.

"Is Jeffrey working today?"

"Yes, I'll be happy to let him know you're here."

It all cleared up like snowy roads in sunshine. Miss Stacey had mentioned her grandson Jeffrey had started working at a tree lot. Candy hadn't paid much attention to the other details, but Mr. Lewiston clearly had.

They waited on the outskirts of the trees near the parking lot. The flakes, which had fallen off and on all morning, had grown larger and more frequent. Flicking one from her cheek, Candy inspected the closest trees and breathed in the smell of fresh pine. Longing filled her. Oh, to take even a small one home. Christmas wouldn't be the same without it. But that wouldn't be today or even this year. She brushed away those thoughts and focused on the task at hand.

Assessing the lot without looking at Mr. Lewiston, she asked, "What kind of tree do you want?"

He shifted next to her. "Something full, like those," he said pointing to a group of lush evergreens. "None of that skinny Charlie Brown nonsense."

Maybe it was her crummy morning that made her feel antagonistic enough to confess her preference. "I happen to like skinny Charlie Brown trees."

He huffed, creating a cloud of breath between them. "Christmas is a grand event." He swung his free arm wide in emphasis. "The tree is the center of it and should represent that fact."

Candy could feel his stern expression as she continued staring at the vast selection. She breathed deep, the fragrance reminding her of forests and happier times. She'd bought a candle once to duplicate the scent, but it never smelled the same.

"No?" Mr. Lewiston asked, apparently unwilling to let it go.

Candy stomped the ground hoping for more circulation to her cold toes while she deliberated her response. "Perhaps Christmas is really about simplicity. Christ wasn't born in a luxury hospital. He was born in a simple stable." She finally looked at him, daring him to contradict her. He seemed at a loss, so she continued. "But if simplicity is what's important then I guess I should just get a fake tree from the drug store."

Mr. Lewiston grew at least two inches. "You will not be putting up an artificial tree."

She couldn't stop the smile or the little ache in her heart. Her grandfather would have said the same thing. "True," she agreed. Maybe she could scavenge some branches from the lot and put them in a vase or along her mantle.

"Do you want your full tree flocked as well?" Candy asked, half expecting him to nod vehemently.

"That just makes a mess. If I want snow on my trees, I'll step outside."

Candy held back a laugh. Before she could think of a

28

witty response, Jeffrey arrived on the scene.

"Mr. Lewiston," he said, holding his hand out for a solid handshake. "Good to see you, sir." He turned to Candy offering his hand. "Jeffrey Niels."

"Candy Kaine." It only took a half a second for the double take. She smiled. "Yep and it's my favorite time of year."

He laughed and apologized, but she just waved it off. She'd had to decide a long time ago not to let it get to her.

"What can I help you find?" Jeffrey asked.

After Mr. Lewiston explained what he wanted, Jeffrey led the way through the rows of trees.

As they walked, Mr. Lewiston said, "We didn't see Miss Stacey at Hearth this morning?" His chin rose with the inflection on the last word.

Jeffrey nodded. Pausing in the aisle he said, "She's been a bit under the weather."

"I hope it isn't the flu," Mr. Lewiston said with an earnest frown.

"No," Jeffrey said shaking his head. "She thought it was a cold, but the doctor says it's pneumonia."

"Oh no," Candy chimed in while Mr. Lewiston stared. "I hope she's getting lots of rest." Candy worried about her like she was one of her patients. "Is she on any antibiotics? Who's taking care of her?"

Jeffrey blinked rapidly.

"Don't mind Candy," Mr. Lewiston said, leaning both hands on his cane. "She is a little excitable sometimes."

Candy felt the unstoppable blush rising up her neck. "I'm so sorry," she said to Jeffrey. She motioned between herself and Mr. Lewiston as she shot the latter a warning look. "We're just really fond of Miss Stacey."

Jeffrey nodded and said, "I think she's on antibiotics. My mom checks in on her before and after work. The doctor just said she needs to take it easy until she's better."

"Do you think she's up for visitors?" Mr. Lewiston asked.

Candy absently stroked the soft pine needles of the nearest tree as the two discussed Miss Stacey's health and possibly visiting.

Mr. Lewiston gestured toward the tree Candy had been admiring and said, "Is that the one you like?"

She laughed as she put her hands behind her back. "The question is, which one do you like?"

"I'm having trouble deciding."

If she picked one, he would disagree and pick something else. Then they could be done and go back to the warmth of the car.

"I think this one is great …"

"But it's got a gap right there," he said pointing to an area of sparse branches.

"You didn't let me finish," Candy teasingly reprimanded. "But I think that one might be perfect." She pointed to a fir a few spots down. "Although, just to be clear, I like the skinny ones better."

Jeffrey pulled it out into the aisle for inspection while Mr. Lewiston hobbled around it. Pausing to scrutinize the tree, the older gentleman reached down and absently rubbed his knee. They probably shouldn't have lingered so long in the cold weather. She hoped *he* didn't get pneumonia.

While Jeffrey arranged for the cut, Candy asked about getting some of the discarded branches.

"Why do you need branches?" asked Mr. Lewiston.

"I like the way they smell and maybe I want to make a wreath."

He eyed her and she defiantly glared back. It was none of his business anyway. He simply nodded.

"Jeffrey, I also need a skinny tree," Mr. Lewiston said as

she gathered a bunch of branches.

Candy held up her hand in a stop-right-now gesture.

"You hate skinny trees."

Mr. Lewiston shrugged and said, "They need a home. You need a tree. Seems like we ought to take care of that while we're here."

Candy's heart sank. This was an expense she hadn't planned on but her pride wouldn't allow her to admit it. She pulled out her purse and Mr. Lewiston cleared his throat.

"My gift to you," he said in a tone that brooked no argument.

"Thank you," she whispered.

Within fifteen minutes Jeffrey and another worker had the trees strapped to the top of Candy's SUV and they were on the road. Candy had longed for a tree but figured having Christmas vicariously through Mr. Lewiston and her other clients was better than none at all. Now, thanks for Mr. Lewiston's generosity, she had a lovely tree.

After a stop at the grocery store, they drove back to Mr. Lewiston's. Excitement and trepidation warred within Candy. She looked forward to helping Mr. Lewiston put up the tree but maybe he would reserve the decoration for the grandkids. Her grandfather always had. At the very least they would get it in the stand and placed, she hoped, in front of the large-paned windows in his living room.

Mr. Lewiston carried a few of the grocery bags in one hand and maneuvered the cane with the other. Candy tagged along behind with the rest. Once the groceries were all put away, Candy said, "Where would you like the tree?"

"We'll need to move a few things around, but it goes right in front of the windows."

The armchair and small table that typically took up the space in front of the windows soon sat off to the side. Candy prepared the tree stand and went to retrieve the grand fir. As she undid the tether, the tree rocked to the side but she grabbed a sturdy branch before it slipped off the car. While steering it to the ground, a branch caught her coat and flipped back, stinging her cheek. She clenched her teeth, biting back the words she wanted to shout at the tree.

After several tries, Candy found a spot she could hold without losing her grip or getting poked in the eye. Dragging it through the snow would have been so much easier, but then it would litter tiny bits of winter all over Mr. Lewiston's living room and he wouldn't like that. As it was, she wiggled between some branches, hoisted it onto her foot, and limped like a one-legged elf late for a hot cider in Santa's lodge.

As soon as she got inside, she shed her coat and sweater. Bringing in the tree had turned into a workout. Banging sounds from the kitchen interrupted her musings on exercise. She balanced the fir against one wall and went to check what was happening. Mr. Lewiston had a pot on the stove and was searching through the cupboard.

"Can I help you find something?"

"No," he said without turning around. "It's a cold day, I'm just going to make some soup. You go work on the tree."

Duly dismissed, she happily returned to her project. Unfortunately, once it appeared straight from one angle, it seemed to lean to another. Finally, she got it looking tall on all sides.

Sizzling sounds and yummy smells of sautéing onions wafted from the kitchen. Mr. Gourmet clearly had a plan other than lunch and she suspected they'd be dropping something off to the ailing Miss Stacey before Candy left for the day. She poked her head in the kitchen and found Mr. Lewiston leaning into the counter and humming as he stirred the contents of the pot.

"Do you want me to get the decorations out?"

"The boxes are in the attic." He glanced up and pointed. "The access is at the end of the hall. Just put them by the tree for the kids. Louise always decorated with them, so they expect that."

Candy retrieved the boxes and the vacuum. Setting the decorations on the couch, she vacuumed the living room. By the time she completed the rest of the housework, Mr. Lewiston had finished his soup and the whole house smelled homey. The ache it created in her heart rolled outward until it consumed every part of her. People who had this were so lucky.

Swallowing the lump in her throat, she said, "Smells delicious."

"Mm. But I think I've made too much." He nodded seriously. "Maybe we should take some over to Miss Stacey since she's feeling under the weather."

"Oh," Candy feigned surprise. "That would be nice. I'm sure she would love that."

"I already packed up a bowl for her." He patted a lidded container.

"Are you ready to take it now or do you want to wait until after lunch?"

"I'm still quite full from breakfast. Let's go now."

***

A woman Candy didn't know answered Miss Stacey's door.

Mr. Lewiston spoke first, "We're friends of Miss Stacey. Wanted to check in on her and bring her some 'magic' soup."

"Oh, come in. I'm Stacey's daughter, Carolyn."

Carolyn took the soup and directed them to Miss Stacey, who sat on the couch watching TV. A couple laughed on screen as they waltzed through the snow. Candy had thought dancing in the rain or snow would be romantic, but Andrew always rushed her to the car claiming he didn't want to catch a cold or he had somewhere to go or someone needed the parking space. She always buried the rejection and gave up asking after a while.

Miss Stacey sat up straighter when she saw them. "Oh, come in. Sit for a spell." Then she ran her hand over her hair. "Oh goodness, I wasn't expecting visitors."

Mr. Lewiston chimed in as he sat in the chair closest to her. "Don't fret now, Miss Stacey, you look absolutely lovely." He shifted his cane. "How are you feeling? We brought some of Louise's magic soup. I probably don't make it like she did, but I hope it'll do the trick."

"I'm sure it will," Miss Stacey said. She leaned over and patted his hand. "I worried about you this morning. Goodness, I hope Patsy took good care of you."

Wanting to give them some space, Candy went to the kitchen to find Carolyn. She wasn't anywhere Candy could see, but the soup sat on the counter.

She poked her head around the corner and asked, "Miss Stacey, would you like me to get you some soup?"

Miss Stacey looked up still smiling. "Oh yes, please, but just a small bowl. My appetite is a bit on the low side."

Candy rummaged through the cupboard and drawers until she found a bowl and a spoon. Luckily there was a tray with a napkin and water glass already on the counter.

The hot soup had cooled perfectly on the drive over. It smelled divine. After pouring a little into the bowl, she tucked the rest into the fridge and refreshed the drink. She returned to the living room where Miss Stacey and Mr.

Lewiston were deep in conversation.

Miss Stacey looked up and said, "Thank you Candy. Oh, isn't that scrumptious?"

Mr. Lewiston rubbed the back of his neck as he cleared his throat. "It isn't much, but we hope it helps you feel better."

The radiant expression told its own story and Candy had no desire to intrude any more on their 'friendship'.

"I'll be in the kitchen. Just let me know when you're ready to go."

Back at Mr. Lewiston's, Candy hurried through the week's food prep. Knowing she was running behind schedule she texted Edie to let her know.

With Mr. Lewiston's dinners labeled and stowed in the fridge, she hurried to the garage for the snow shovel. It only took a few minutes to clear the walk. She said good-bye to Mr. Lewiston and headed back into the gloomy afternoon. The storm had left only a few inches on the ground, so the drive home was uneventful, aside from the clouds parting just as the sun dropped behind the mountains. The colorful sky seemed a token of cheer although it ended before she pulled into her garage.

Several inches of fresh snow covered the path to Edie's but it easily brushed to the sides as Candy swept the path. Leaving the broom on the porch, she knocked and opened the door without waiting.

"Hey Edie, it's me, Candy."

Edie appeared a moment later, hopping along and using the wall as a support. Her fracture boot was nowhere to be seen.

"Edie? Where's your boot?"

"Don't worry about the boot, dear. I'm just so glad you made it safely here. I was a bit worried. Pacing in that

35

contraption bothered me so I took it off."

Candy checked out Edie's ankle. Making some adjustments to the boot she encouraged her to wear it and not to walk on it too much yet. They chatted while Candy threw together a quick chicken and rice stir-fry.

"You know I love having you visit, dear, but I sure will be glad to be back on my feet and able to make my own dinner again."

"You'll be good as new in no time," Candy said. "As long as you take care of yourself. If you don't, then I'll be making your dinners and driving you around a lot longer."

"You know, my grandson Jace used to make a mean Dutch oven dinner."

Here we go again. Mr. Perfect.

Of course he made a mean Dutch oven dinner. It went with his fabulous cast iron biscuits. Candy nodded her head, perhaps a bit too enthusiastically. Envy snaked through her. She'd longed to impress her dad with her culinary abilities and had tried using the Dutch oven from his camping gear. It had been the worst dinner. Ever. She cringed at the memory.

"Maybe next time he's here, he could give me some tips," she said too cheerfully.

"He wouldn't want me saying so, but …" Edie leaned in and whispered, "My favorite is his cobbler."

This eased the tension. Candy laughed at the shared 'secret', suspecting it was because cobbler was too feminine.

"Why would he care that you say that?"

"Oh, you know. Cobbler isn't very manly. But there's nothing that compares, in my opinion."

"True, who doesn't love a good cobbler?" Her mouth watered at the thought of juicy peaches simmering in gooey syrup with a sprinkle of cinnamon and a crumb topping.

They ate together and talked a bit more about Edie's two

grandkids. Edie's shoulders hunched and she pushed the food around her plate.

"What's wrong, Edie?"

"Oh nothing."

"Don't like my dinner?"

Edie stared down, seeming surprised to find the food at the end of her fork. She gave a wry laugh and said, "It's not that, it's just that it seems so long since the grandkids have come home for Christmas." She sighed. The fried rice moved in full submission to the swirling of her fork. "We used to do all kinds of things like decorate gingerbread houses and make hot cocoa and play dodge the mistletoe."

"Dodge the mistletoe?"

A tiny smile lit Edie's face. "I would hang the mistletoe in a different place everyday and when I caught them standing under it, I would smother them in kisses." The smile turned to sadness. "They grew out of that pretty quickly."

A little pain flared in Candy's chest. Didn't her grandkids know how much all of this meant to her? She made a mental note of gingerbread houses and decorations and determined to do what she could to make up for the absence of Edie's grandchildren.

After a quick clean of the kitchen, Candy returned to her own home.

Chapter 4

Rather than feeling better after talking to his grandmother, Jace's frustration amped up. Instead of pacing, he began an upper body workout routine using his own weight as resistance.

His mind wandered to Raxoco Resorts as he counted reps. They needed a temporary web designer to manage the advertising and launch pages for their newest acquisition-in-progress. The building sat nestled at the base of a small hill in Jace's hometown. The details of the property had faded with the eight years he'd been gone. Unfortunately, he may need to go back to get a feel for the building, its best side, some interior shots, and other things that would appeal to high-end clientele. Things he shouldn't worry about unless he got the job.

If it worked out and he did well, it could finally get his career moving forward again. If not, well, he didn't want to think about the coming eviction notice or the power shutting off. Nor did he want to think about more ramen noodles or crawling back home at twenty-six, begging for a place to stay and a job on his dad's construction crew until he got back on his feet.

But more than that, he didn't want Liz to be right. When he'd ended their relationship several months ago, she had said a lot of things, but what stuck in his head was that he "'would never amount to anything." In retribution, she had worked his client list to almost nothing. She'd closed those doors just as she'd opened them. He sighed.

Fifteen-hour workdays hadn't enabled him to keep up with the lavish life she expected. He had enjoyed it at first, but working to impress people who were only impressed by a financial statement wore thin after a while. When he'd said they needed to cut back, she'd thrown a major tantrum demanding a diamond tennis bracelet as an apology for his insensitivity.

The next day, on his way to the jewelry store, he drove past a park. A couple of older people shared a bench there, googley-eyeing each other over a sack lunch. Liz would never go for a sack lunch date. If he'd even had the nerve to suggest it, she would have demanded to know what had possessed him and then pouted until the appropriate number of bouquets had arrived. And he never knew how many. Once, it had gone on for two weeks.

And she'd never looked at him like that either. Ever. She might have looked at him sweetly, but only when she wanted something. It surprised him that he wanted what that elderly couple had—old-fashioned love. But that was a thing of the past. The current culture of couples seemed to have benefits without commitment and certainly without mutual respect and loyalty. The car behind him had honked and something about that and the couple jarred him. He had turned the car around and returned to Liz's apartment knowing he would be walking into a firestorm.

The cell phone on the coffee table buzzed, bringing him back to the present. Caller ID said Raxoco Resorts. His heart pounded in his chest. This was it. He needed to still his breathing and sound confident. Taking a deep breath, he answered.

"Jace Marlowe speaking."

"Mr. Marlowe, this is Liesl Thomas, Raxoco Resorts," she greeted in a tone more friendly than businesslike. His hopes soared.

"Good afternoon, Ms. Thomas." He hated how much he sounded like his dad, but he didn't think a 'hey Liesl' would go over well. He really needed this, even if it was temporary.

"Please, call me Liesl," her voice purred. Maybe he'd been wrong. She continued, "You know I'm pulling for you, but the Board of Directors is still undecided on whether we need your services at this time."

The way she said 'services' sent a chill tapping down his spine. He shook it off. Now was not the time to pick and choose jobs.

"Do they have any specific concerns I can address?"

"No." Short. Clipped. She didn't offer any details.

He fished. "What can I do to help the process along?"

"Andrew, go get me a coffee." The curt order caught him off guard but before he could respond, she said in a confidential whisper, "Sometimes he's a little too attentive." Her tone had warmed again. Jace could hear what sounded like a pen tapping on the desk. "Maybe we could get together for drinks tonight," she said. "You know, go over a strategy, and get the weekend started."

Whoa. In his head, warning bells rang like air raid sirens. How would it come across if he said he couldn't afford to 'wine and dine' her?

"Ah, Ms. Thomas."

His brain refused to work fast enough. Bad excuses fell all over themselves as the good ones hid in the shadows.

"Liesl."

"Liesl, then." He closed his eyes, inhaled, and said what he hoped would come across as professional. "I generally don't mix business and pleasure." He mentally kicked himself. Could he get any more cliché?

"Generally?" She seemed to cling to the loophole he'd left open. "Well, Raxoco is interested in you. It would be unfortunate if you could not make an exception." She paused, the silence spinning for a moment like the colorful pinwheel of death before she continued, "I was hoping you'd be more of a ..." She paused. "Team player."

What could it hurt? Except he had no money to pay for it. Every credit card he owned would be declined. And he was pretty sure that would get him kicked off 'the team.'

"I probably could make an exception." He would have to beg some money from his buddy Ladd and that would require explaining things he didn't want to divulge.

"Excellent."

A dirge played ominously in the back of his head. How could he get out of this? Maybe if he called the shots.

"Let's meet at Lou's BBQ at seven o'clock."

Lou's was a busy, sawdust-on-the-floor, beer-on-tap kind of place that served up better barbecue than a church potluck in the Bible Belt.

"Well ..." The word came out long and smothered in distaste. "I was actually thinking The Marble Gardens."

He hadn't been there since his days with Liz. It had its appeal at first. Eventually, though, the facade hiding the ugly nature of those who frequented it faded. Going back would be like selling his soul.

"That's my ex's favorite place and I'd rather not run into her." Who could argue with that?

"Oh? Maybe I know her."

He didn't like where this was going, but his brainpower had been poured into a web page today.

"I hope not. She doesn't have anything nice to say about me." Again, the truth. Wasn't he supposed to be skirting that topic and promoting his abilities to do this job? "How about The Plaid Tycoon?" Upscale, but not elegant.

"I guess that would be fine. I'll see you at seven then."

Jace sat on the stool and dropped his head into his hands, wiping away the sweat that had beaded there. It was sixty-something degrees in his apartment, so how was he sweating? Not a good sign. Maybe he was overreacting, mistaking Liesl's tone for something it wasn't. But his gut said different. He thought of Liz and all her deception and the way she had played him. He wasn't completely innocent either. Her connections had given him immediate success, but it had come with its price. He refused to go down that path again even if it left him homeless. The Board was going to have to make a decision without this little meeting tonight.

He dialed the number Liesl had used to call him.

"Raxoco Resorts. This is Andrew. How may I assist you?"

"Hi, Andrew, it's Jace Marlowe. I just spoke with Ms. Thomas. Is she available by any chance?"

A fraction of silence passed before Andrew spoke.

"One moment please."

Jace waffled again, after all, it was just drinks. He should probably go. He needed this gig. Desperately.

"Jace?"

Her voice was husky. It was a Liz voice, attempting to use her appeal to get what she wanted. The air in the room thickened. He shook his head, even though she couldn't see it.

"I apologize, Ms. Thomas ..."

"I thought we agreed on Liesl."

Jace cringed at the clipped tone. May as well get it over with.

"Okay. Well, I called to let you know I won't be able to meet after all."

She said nothing, perhaps waiting for him to change his mind. But he wouldn't.

"That's unfortunate. I guess we'll wait and see what the Board has to say after the Monday morning meeting."

"Thanks for understanding," He said even though he knew she didn't. "I look forward to talking again on Monday. Have a good weekend, Liesl."

Jace stared out the tiny kitchen window. He'd just ruined the biggest opportunity he'd had in a long time, maybe ever. The sky, grim and dreary, matched his mood. The darkening of the late afternoon pressed in on him. This hole he was in might consume him.

Pull yourself together, Jace. Look for the good.

He got to stay home tonight. That was a good thing. Weather forecasters had predicted sleet turning to snow overnight. He avoided driving in that kind of weather whenever possible. Sliding off the road and rolling his dad's truck in high school had cured that.

He had a roof over his head and a mattress to sleep on. Both good things. Although maybe not for long with rent due tomorrow. He did have a part-time seasonal job and he could pick up his check tomorrow, but it would only cover two weeks of rent.

His phone buzzed as a new text popped up.

STILL HAVE THE COFFEE TABLE?

And if he could sell that, he could grab some groceries and squeak out this month's rent. Good things.

They negotiated back and forth agreeing to meet at a central location because of the storm. In between those messages he sent a text to Ladd asking if he could bring his truck and help move the beastly thing. Jace and the buyer settled on a price and a pick-up time. Ladd had agreed to come. By the time he arrived, Jace had the coffee table halfway out his apartment door.

Ladd, never one to miss the obvious, said, "Dude, what happened? You have *no* furniture."

"Not true. I have a kitchen stool. And a mattress."

Ladd's eyes narrowed and he put his hand on the coffee table stalling Jace's progress. "What's going on, Jace?"

Their friendship had started at college, had survived dating and job changes, but when Liz had come along, he'd put all of his friendships on hold.

"Things are a little tight, that's all."

"It's more than that. You're a college graduate. In computer systems." Ladd's eyes now opened wide. "This is because of that crowd you were hanging with, isn't it? You got into that scene and now you can't get out. You're snorting everything you make."

Jace held up a hand. "No. Not even close. You should know me better than that."

"I don't know which Jace you are. The Liz Jace or the Jace I knew in college who always had some philanthropic thing going on."

"Neither I guess."

"Then where's all your money going?"

"There's no money coming in." Jace glared. Why did Ladd have to be so pushy? "When you dump an influential businessman's daughter and she has a vendetta," he finally admitted, "It doesn't matter if you're the best in the industry."

He glanced up at the sky. Sleet had started falling, pinging off the covered parking. It would likely escalate as the night went on.

"Let's get this loaded before the storm gets worse."

They carried it down the stairs and to Ladd's truck. Instead of asking more questions, Ladd grabbed a couple of blankets from behind the driver's seat. One went under and the other covered the coffee table. They secured the table and climbed in.

As they left to meet the buyer Ladd started to interrogate

again.

"What about next month? It doesn't look like you have anything left to sell. Except maybe your car."

"I'm working on in it. Had a job interview today." Jace shook his head at the memory.

"Apparently it didn't go well?"

"I won't know until Monday, but yeah, not counting on it."

"Why don't you get out of here? Move to another city?"

"I've got two more months on my lease, so I'm here for at least that long."

Ladd glanced over. "You don't live in the cheap rent district either."

"Nope, but I'm the fool that signed the lease." He stared into the night. He had been a fool. A very big fool trying to fast track his success.

"Sorry, man. That's rough," Ladd said. "If you get tossed, you can always crash at my place for a couple of days. But you've got to figure this out."

"Thanks, Dad."

Ladd laughed. Jace was relieved that he talked about other things on the short drive to deliver the table. Afterward, they'd gone to Lou's BBQ to grab dinner. Jace had savored every bite.

When they pulled back into the complex parking lot, Ladd tapped the steering wheel. Jace hoped he wouldn't bring up their earlier conversation. But Ladd faced him and said, "I know things aren't ideal. If you need a loan, let me know."

Earlier tonight, he'd contemplated that very thing, but now, if he was very careful, he could make it to the end of December.

"Thanks." He held up the envelope of cash. "This will get me through for a while."

"I'll talk to my dad and see if he has any leads, maybe he can get the word out."

"Oh, the word's out. No need to worry there."

Jace leaned his head back. It was so frustrating to be in the spot he swore he wouldn't go back to. Ladd was right. There was nothing left to sell. Except his car.

"You know what I mean."

"Thanks. You're a good friend, even though I haven't been." He didn't like this place where he was, but also didn't know how to get out of it.

"Dude, you'll make it. You're one of the smartest guys I know. Just promise me you'll let me know if you need help."

Jace nodded. "Thanks. It means a lot."

He was loath to go back to his cold, empty apartment, but the wind had picked up and the sleet had turned to a million tiny snowflakes. Better for Ladd if he didn't have to drive in it with the chance of it worsening. Jace said goodbye, then jogged through the storm replaying the conversation all the way back to his apartment. He *would* make it.

Once the computer was on, he searched Internet job sites for new possibilities. The company where he'd done a summer internship during college had posted a job. It wasn't really what he was looking for, but it would be a start. He sent off the application and his resume and continued looking.

As he scrolled, a couple of options caught his interest. Both needed work to update their current sites. One was a pet shelter with a picture of a boxer that looked like his childhood dog, Wags. The brown, pleading eyes hooked him and without a second thought he sent the required information.

The other was a children's museum and activity center. If he could land a couple of paying jobs, he would offer to do

46

both site updates for free. As soon as he thought it, though, the guilt began gnawing at him. The right thing would be to do it without expectation of anything in return. But what about keeping a roof over his head? And keeping the heat on? Those things seemed pretty essential. He toggled between the two pages, his heart going out to the kids and the dogs. The ways he could help were limited, but not impossible. He sent an e-mail to both, offering to do the work pro bono. It would be a good way to add to his portfolio.

Upon further perusal of the jobs available, he found three more that interested him. He sent his resume and links to his work and hoped for the best.

Chapter 5

Saturday flew by with the morning hours spent either studying or job hunting for something that accommodated a college schedule. Candy considered moving back over the mountain, but that would have to be her last option. Right now, she would scrape up what few seasonal jobs she could find, like coordinating the VIP tickets and schedule for the upcoming Christmas Chorale. The tickets had gone on sale that morning and over half were already reserved.

The VIP seating, besides being the first five rows of pews, included a champagne and light hors d'oeuvres meet and greet with the Mayor, Town Council, and Chorale committee, a 'Friends of the Chorale' mention in the program, and a CD recording of the production. Most people signed up on the website, but she still got a few phone calls with questions or special accommodation requests.

She loved her caregiving jobs for the most part, but coordinating the VIP event was a nice change. And it perfectly filled her schedule. She wouldn't be too busy while she had finals, but the majority of work would come the week of the Chorale, when she had more time on her hands than she wanted. Time meant contemplation about her life, something she'd avoided since the breakup. So she worked long hours, studied even longer, and avoided getting too close to anyone.

Candy had worked the afternoon at the care center. Residents in the assisted living wing kept her running the whole time. The exhausting shift left her with no desire to cook, so she grabbed burgers for her and Edie at the only drive-thru in town. The extra hours she would pick up once the semester ended would ease her tight budget.

48

"Hello," Candy called as she let herself in to Edie's.

Edie hobbled from the kitchen. "Oh, there you are. I wasn't sure if you were coming. I was just poking through the fridge."

"I know it isn't your favorite, but I brought burgers and fries."

Edie grimaced as expected, so Candy said, "There's salad in the crisper."

She retrieved it along with some salad dressing. Edie made her way to the table, wincing as she went.

"Edie," Candy said concern lacing her voice. "What's wrong? Are you in pain?"

"Just my body reminding me how old I am. "

"You're not really old, you know. Old is like maybe ninety-four," Candy said as she pulled out a couple of plates.

"Tell that to the vacuum."

Stunned, Candy's said, "I can help with cleaning until you get back on your feet. Right now, that fractured foot needs you to take care."

Edie waved her off as she sat in her usual spot at the table.

"I'll be fine tomorrow, dear. Besides, I can't be hobbling around church. Mrs. Tarrington would have a hay day with that. She's already saying I'm faking it so I have an excuse not to decorate."

Candy chuckled. Welcome to Small-Town, USA. She put a plate in front of Edie and sat across from her. They held hands and Edie said grace.

When Edie finished praying, Candy asked, "Did you actually hear Mrs. Tarrington say that?"

"No, but Janice did."

"Well, we can't worry about what Mrs. Tarrington does or says. It doesn't change anything anyway."

"Well, if my kids or grandkids would give a care, maybe

49

they could make time to come see an old woman before she's dust in the ground." Edie's frown lengthened to a forced smile. She leaned back, away from Candy. "Don't you have some homework or project to run off to tonight?" She asked sarcastically.

Candy clenched her jaw. "Well, I certainly can pack up my dinner and take it home. Would you like me to do that?"

Edie had the decency to look abashed. "No, dear." It lasted all of two seconds and the frown returned. "But don't let me keep you from your *important* life."

"Edie!"

Candy smacked the table with her palm and then stood, pushing her chair away. She did not need this aggravation. Edie's hand, clenching a burger, paused halfway to her mouth. Her eyes widened.

Deep breath in, two, three, four and out, two, three, four.

"Edie. I understand you are upset, but you may not talk to me like that. I actually finished most of my homework yesterday so that I could stay longer with you tonight. However, there's always plenty I can study. You decide."

Edie put her burger back on her plate and stared at it. Candy felt like she was lecturing a five-year-old. Returning to her seat, she stabbed a chunk of lettuce and started eating.

Candy had eaten most of her food when Edie finally broke the silence between them.

"It would be nice if you stayed, but I understand if you have to rush home."

"I can stay. What would you like to do?"

"I've got an old Dickens Christmas puzzle. It's five thousand pieces. Usually it takes me all of December, but we could get started on it. It's at the top of the hall closet," Edie said hopefully.

"Perfect," Candy said. She took their dishes to the sink.

"Would you like it on the kitchen table or do you prefer a card table?"

"Here will be fine," Edie said patting the spot in front of her. "There's a rolled up plastic covering that goes over it when we're not working on it. It's in the spare room closet."

Candy returned with both and began setting up. Small talk dotted their work for a couple of hours until all the pieces faced up. They hadn't even started putting the edge together. No wonder it took the whole month to finish. Candy couldn't believe how fast the time went.

"I'm going to clean up the kitchen and then I've got to get going," she said. "What time would you like me to pick you up for services in the morning?"

"Nine-thirty would be fine, dear."

At home she wrapped up the last of her homework and checked her e-mail. It looked like her dad had e-mailed her, but upon opening it discovered Andrew had sent it using an alias similar to her dad's. She hated to change her e-mail address, but it looked like that was where this would end. It wasn't a nice message and although she figured he had been drinking, it still made her cringe every time she thought about it. Climbing into bed, she was grateful, again, that she'd ended things.

It had been a long time since she'd attended church regularly. This Sunday's service was nice and she felt a peace that had evaded her since her breakup with Andrew. The pastor rambled on about the commandment to love God and to love your neighbor. She thought about her own situation. She did love God, although she'd abandoned Him. And she did love Mr. Lewiston and her neighbors. But what about other people in her life? For the first time in nine months, she admitted to herself that she carried a lot of bitterness in her heart toward myriad people from her life before Saint Angelo.

What if? What if she returned to God? What if she forgave those people? What if she gave that burden to Christ? Moved on. Healed. It all sounded good in theory, but she wasn't strong enough to do that. It was an old worn blanket that she wasn't willing to part with just yet.

Those thoughts troubled her the rest of the day. Sitting through Edie's Christmas Chorale practice didn't ease the discomfort. Even helping a few people get their tickets for the performance did nothing for her morale. She immersed herself in studying until the rehearsal finished.

The temperatures had dropped at least fifteen degrees since they'd entered the church an hour and a half ago and the over-warm air of the church made the outside chill even more pronounced. The sun had moved on with its weak light, leaving frigid air and darkness. A fitting way to end the day.

"Edie, why don't you wait inside while I get the car?"

Edie wrapped her scarf around her head and hobbled farther out into the night.

"No need to do that. I'm not afraid of whatever Jackie Frost can throw our way." She chuckled softly as if she'd made some private joke.

The car was parked too far for the remote to work, but Candy tried the automatic start button anyway. Nothing. They shuffled along, making a path in the tiny ice crystals blanketing the sidewalk. As soon as she thought the remote would work, she tried again. This time, the engine roared to life. Relief filled her. Maybe by the time they got there it would be a tiny bit warmer.

Candy walked with one hand in her pocket and one arm through Edie's. When they finally reached the car, Edie maneuvered herself into the passenger seat and Candy stowed their handbags in the back. A shiver racked her body as she reached her door. Even with the heaters and seat warmers on, she still felt the chill all the way home.

The alarm clock blared the next morning much sooner than Candy wanted. Tossing and turning all night had made it even more difficult to get up. She reached an arm out and turned off the alarm.

Monday classes started at nine o'clock, which meant there was no time to laze about in bed. A few minutes later, dressed and seated in an armchair near the again-blazing fire, she sipped her tea and checked her e-mail.

There were only a few messages. The first one she opened was from her psychology teacher.

I've awarded you 10 bonus points on Quiz 5. Your assessment of Hitler is arguable. The points are for thinking and responding.

Hadn't she deleted that answer? The crazy morning last week had thrown her off-schedule, so really anything was possible. But wait, she simply needed to answer those impossible questions? Why hadn't he just said so? It reminded her of something he said frequently during class about failure only existing for those who quit. Apparently, that extended to his quizzes as well as life. A grin crept across her face. This meant she had a chance to keep her academic scholarship.

The next e-mail was forwarded from her student account at Mack Community College. It was from Financial Services.

We regret to inform you that all scholarships for students

53

attending classes at satellite locations will be suspended at the end of Fall semester. If you would like to explore other scholarship options, please contact a counselor in our office.

The elation evaporated. Her chest tightened and the living room seemed to shrink around her. It hadn't mattered that her grade point average would stay above 3.5. Stretching out both arms she mentally pushed against the anxiety. It wasn't the end of the world or even her college classes. She would find a way to make it work. Except the 'how' part of that determination, eluded her. She brought her arms in to hug herself.

Closing her eyes, she took a deep breath in an attempt to ease the panic. The choices were so limited, but like her psych professor said, failure is giving up. Another deep breath. She could do this. She would go see her counselor after her nursing class at the main campus this week. As an afterthought she sent up a little plea to God. On that note, Candy checked the last of the e-mails.

Hey beautiful. I haven't heard back from you. You know you'll never find something as good as we had, so I'm psyched to come to Saint Angie. I've been super busy with this project I'm working on but I've had that song 'I want Candy' running through my head all weekend. Looking forward to a sweet sugar rush when we get together. Still working on final plans, but Monday night is still a go. See you then.

This note was much nicer than the last one, but still. Ugh. She didn't want to deal with him. Deleting the message, she rubbed her temples, hoping to release the building tension. Would anything go right this morning?

Chapter 6

Jace had spent the weekend updating his personal website and reaching out to past clients. And checking his e-mail. By late Sunday, both the children's home and the shelter had tentatively accepted his offer. Jace sent over a contract with the fees waived. He was excited to get to work on the projects and would request recommendations on professional social media sites once the jobs were complete. That might begin to undo the damage Liz had done. Unfortunately two of the paying jobs had declined and the other hadn't responded.

A couple of energy bars were the only things in the cupboard. He ate one for breakfast Monday morning with the last of the milk. He couldn't even afford to brew a cup of coffee these days. His phone buzzed on the kitchen counter. Raxoco Resorts. His heart sank. He couldn't endure any more bad news.

"Jace Marlowe speaking."

"Mr. Marlowe, it's Andrew, Ms. Thomas's assistant." She couldn't even do her own dirty work, her office boy had to call and turn him down.

"Good morning, Andrew."

"I'm calling to tell you Raxoco Resorts would like to offer you that web design job."

Stunned by this turn of luck, Jace sat silent.

"Mr. Marlowe?"

"Yes, sorry, it's Monday morning. Long weekend."

"Dude, I hear you. When we're in Saint Angelo in a couple a weeks, we'll get my girlfriend to hook you up and we can all go out." He paused for a moment. "That is, if you'll accept the job."

No thank you on the hookups. That had never been his thing. But as the news of the offer sunk in, Jace jumped up and fist-pumped the air. The impossible had just flipped to possible.

Andrew continued, "It's a great gig."

It could be, Jace knew, but remembering his conversation with Ms. Thomas, it could also crash his future plans. Andrew droned on something about one of the girls in the office.

"Liesl is definitely great to work with … Anyway, if you're game, she would like you to send over the contract so the attorney can review it."

"I have a few things to take care of this morning." Nothing pressing, but Jace wanted to sound like people sought his work. "But I can send it out this afternoon and you can contact me with any questions." His voice sounded much calmer than the exhilaration careening through his veins. He couldn't believe how things had turned around.

"Awesome, man. Once it's reviewed, we'll get back to you … probably by close of business tomorrow."

"That should work out fine. I have a couple of other projects I'm currently working on, but once we get the contract details worked out, Raxoco will be a priority."

"I'll let Liesl know. She likes to be a 'priority'." His emphasis on priority made Jace uneasy.

"Also, Liesl and I will be traveling to Saint Angelo the week before Christmas." Andrew hesitated and Jace sensed tension but Andrew continued without explaining. "She expects you to join us. Raxoco will pay for the hotel and you'll have a per diem for other expenses."

Ideally, Jace would have preferred staying at the resort, but it didn't exist yet. He also learned from Andrew that the manor house slated for purchase currently accommodated a satellite campus for Mack Community College.

Wait. His mind raced. That was the old Janssen Manor. They'd done a tour of it as a senior class. The counselors had encouraged students to attend. His best friend Ty, who wanted to study architecture, could not stop pointing out things like pillars and hand-carved molding. He'd droned on and on about a bunch of stuff that Jace didn't understand or care about. But now, all those details would be perfect for this project.

Andrew interrupted Jace's thoughts saying classes would finish the second week of December and then, that third week their group would have access to the grounds. Fortunately for Raxoco, Ms. Thomas had a connection to someone on the college's board. They had gotten carte blanche access for that week and had been all but guaranteed the sale. And, according to Andrew, although there were other hotels and vacant properties located nearby, none had the same potential.

"Sounds like she's got all the bases covered."

"Yes, she does." Again, Andrew's tone soured.

Jace hesitated, but, desperate for the cash flow the job would provide, he jumped right back in. "Thanks Andrew."

"Sure thing, man. It's going to be great having you on the team."

Andrew's tone was a long way from convincing Jace he really felt that way but Jace did a little victory dance around the empty living room anyway.

Excited and nervous about returning to his hometown, Jace logged on and searched hotel properties in Saint Angelo, including the new Hotel Lush, where Andrew said they had reservations. He wanted to explore their web pages as well as check out where they would be staying.

Grandma Edie still lived in Saint Angelo. This would be a

great opportunity to surprise her with a visit. He'd talked to her every Sunday since he'd graduated high school and left the small town eight years ago. Eight years. More than half of it spent on degrees from the state university, the other portion scraping up jobs to pay off student loans, the rent, and the high-end lifestyle that he hadn't cared for. The longer he thought about surprising her, the more excited he became. She always told him to come visit, but he always had a reason to stay away. This year would be different.

The church his family had attended during his growing up years always hosted a Christmas Chorale. They invited a couple of other local church choirs and the theater company to participate.

It was usually a few weeks before Christmas. Every past year, Grandma Edie had looked forward to singing with the Chorale and Jace figured this year would be no different. Except this year, he could show up without her knowing and be one of her raving fans when it was all over, toting flowers and everything. But he had no idea where to start planning for something like that. Of course, the website would have some information, but he couldn't remember the exact name of the church.

Another quick search brought up the town's homepage including a link to information on the Christmas Chorale. It had the date listed as December 15 at 7:00 p.m. Less than two weeks away. Perfect timing. He could spend a week there, working, skiing, and catching up with his grandma.

He scrolled down the page to find the link to ticket purchases. A 'sold out' banner covered the link for General Admission. For VIP admission, the site listed a couple of phone numbers. One was for Alice Raleigh. Jace had thought her old when he was a kid—and if he remembered correctly, she wasn't one to keep things to herself, so she was

definitely out. There was also a Candice Krane listed.
Perhaps he would call her this morning. After several
minutes of vacillating between calling Ms. Krane or skipping
the Chorale and just showing up, Jace shoved his nerves
aside and dialed the number listed.

While it rang, he clicked over to his inbox. Instead of the
list of e-mails he expected, a server error page came up. His
heart sank. Not this, too. He clicked around and two things
happened simultaneously. He discovered his Internet really
wasn't working and a female voice interrupted the ringing
phone with a cheery "Hello."

More forcefully than he intended he said, "Candice." It
wasn't even a question. He'd meant to be polite and call her
Ms. Krane, but his brain and mouth hadn't communicated.
All that came through was his frustration over his downed
Internet. She didn't answer and he thought maybe his cell
service had crashed as well.

After a few seconds she said, "I'll admit, I'm stunned at
your audacity." An underlying tremor warbled through her
voice. Before he could respond, there was an audible intake
of breath and she continued. "You think you can come here
for a weekend and everything will be forgiven? That you can
make up for your indiscretions, your high-flying lifestyle
with flowers and dinner and your smooth talking? Well,
think again because nothing will change. Nothing. Don't call
me again." After some muffled sounds and a thump her
distant voice said, "Stupid men."

Jace stared at the phone. His nostrils flared as heat
coursed through his body. Stupid men? How about stupid
women?

She had no idea how stifling that place had been for him,
for his dreams. He'd left with no plans of ever going back
and this short trip would be just that, short. Barely long

enough to visit Grandma Edie and get this job done. He would not go back to St. A on any other terms. Ever. And just to be clear, a day on the slopes didn't count as a high-flying lifestyle. It was one of the only perks that existed in St. A.

Things had looked up during his brief phone call with Andrew but now the pendulum swung the other direction. He stood and paced, still breathing too fast, too shallow. How did she even know who he was?

He stopped pacing as it hit him. His name must have shown on her caller ID. Eight years apparently wasn't long enough to erase the rebellious and painful teenage years.

Memories of pounding nails and being last for everything because you're the boss's son or you lived on the wrong street streamed like a bad movie trailer. Ms. Krane had probably been fed with a silver spoon her entire life with no idea what hard work was. What did she know about his life? Nothing, that's what. Perhaps they had misspelled her name and it should be Krank.

Running his fingers through his already mussed hair, he drew in a deep breath. And another, blowing it out slowly. Calling for VIP tickets was clearly out. Maybe he could get Andrew to get some. But then there was the possibility that Andrew and Liesl would want to accompany him and he didn't want his past put on display for them. He wondered briefly if Ms. Krank would be any nicer to Andrew or if she reserved that for anyone who hadn't visited his grandmother in eight years. Nothing was secret in small towns. Besides, Grandma came once a month to shop and visit. He had figured that was enough. He'd called often, but hated the thought of returning, of being reminded of his insignificance, as if by going back he wouldn't be able to escape again.

Chapter 7

Candy surveyed the skies as she left her afternoon shift at Senior Living at The Pines. The week was half over, and snow had fallen intermittently every day. Today had proven different only in the constant and larger snowflakes. She drove at a deliberate pace on the narrow, snow-packed streets. The last thing she needed was Darwin the Tow Guy pulling her out of another snowbank. If the last time's 'accidental' touching hadn't put her off, the bawdy jokes and pressure to go out with him would have. She shivered just thinking about it. To be fair, her Jeep could have gotten her out all on its own, Darwin just happened to be right behind her when it happened and had his tow line hooked up before she had the sense to object.

The forecast had called for minimal snow until the weekend, but Mother Nature apparently had other ideas. Candy hoped it would clear up overnight so the drive to the city for her Thursday nursing class wouldn't be too awful. She mentally planned an extra thirty minutes for the next morning's drive.

After pulling into her driveway, she ended up shoveling her way over to Edie's. There was no way the wet snow would be swept away today.

She found Edie, boot off, trying to climb a ladder to the attic.

"Ah, Edie! What are you doing?"

"I know, dear. I should have waited for you, but I really wanted to get these decorations set up. Everywhere we go, there's cheer and festive spirits and the Christmas movie I was watching had a red berry wreath like mine and I just couldn't wait any longer."

Her smile of chagrin melted Candy's anger away.

"Aren't the Christmas boxes in the garage?"

"Oh, those? They're the outside decorations. Henry and Jace always took care of those." A hint of sadness hitched her voice when she mentioned Henry.

Wanting Edie to focus on the excitement from a moment ago, Candy said, "Well, I'm here now, so let me grab the ones from the attic and you can start getting things out." She looked up the ladder. Edie's small figure swayed across the dark opening to the attic as she turned and made her way down.

"They're in the green bins with the red lids," she said, moving out of the way.

Candy climbed up until her torso cleared the attic door. The limited light from below barely illuminated the small space. A box marked 'Easter' sat on top of another one with a big red heart scrawled on it. Next to those were stacked several dark bins. Hunched over to avoid smacking her head on the beams, she crept toward the bins and pulled them within reaching distance of the opening. Back out on the ladder she handed the bins to Edie, who stacked them neatly in the hallway.

"The tree box is up there too."

Candy did a visual search, but didn't see anything, so crawled back into the space.

"Is there a light up here, Edie? I'm not seeing a tree box." Something brushed against her cheek. She jerked back, swatting at the air. Her heart pounded. Surely some spider had taken up residence and would now torment her because she'd invaded its space. Looking more closely, she discovered, not the expected cobweb, but the light cord. She laughed at her skittishness and pulled the string.

Click.

Nothing.

"Edie, the light's burned out, do you have an extra bulb?"

Minutes later a new bulb lit the attic and Candy saw the tree box tucked toward the eaves. She pulled it out and lowered it down the stairs.

The artificial tree had required a bit of work before the lights twinkled on every bough. But now, hours later, a small train chugged around the tiny village under the branches. The red berry wreath hung from the brass hook on the front door and various Santas and Nutcrackers were interspersed with the knick-knacks on shelves and tables. A large papier-mâché nativity occupied the coffee table. Edie opened the last of the bins and pulled out a large, tattered box. Once opened, it produced another holy family. From the looks of the box, it had seen a lot of Christmases.

"This one is for you, dear," Edie said.

Candy pushed the box containing the nativity back toward the elderly woman. "Edie, I can't take that, it looks like a family heirloom." Besides, other than the pine branches and the tree Mr. Lewiston had bought her, she wasn't decorating her own home, wasn't joining the festive season—not because she didn't want to, but she'd discovered that she missed the family aspect and that had soured her today.

"It isn't a gift. You're just borrowing it." Edie said. "And I can tell you need some Christmas cheer. I think this is just the thing."

The warm smile that accompanied the offer carried a hint of mischief. Curiosity nearly undid Candy, but she drew in a steadying breath and said, "I don't need Christmas cheer. I'll be fine without it."

"You don't believe, then?"

"Of course I believe." She hated her own pettiness and steered the conversation away from it. "I believe toy

63

companies and retail outlets have sabotaged the true spirit of Christmas and I want none of it," she said with a dramatic sweep of her arm.

She hoped the declaration would divert Edie from needing to fill her month of December with, as Edie put it, cheer. Christmas was about Christ, she knew that, but after the wedding fiasco, her belief had dissipated to barely there.

"Nonsense." Edie's already thin lips drew into a line. "Sometimes, we cannot see past our disbelief." She put the box on top of Candy's bag. "If you do believe, you will take this home and set it out. It has nothing to do with commercialism." Then she looked out the front windows and sighed. "It's too bad my Jace isn't here, he could string the lights outside."

With that announcement, she hobbled over to the couch, where she unceremoniously plopped down. "I'm going to watch TV. Why don't you sit with me for a bit?"

Candy knew what that meant, whether it was advertising or the latest movie: romance and Christmas. Gah. She may as well be forced to poke her own eyes out and stuff cotton in her ears. Maybe the nativity wasn't such a bad option at this point. Or the lights.

"Where are your lights? I'll put them up for you."

Edie waved her off. "You don't have to do that, dear. Maybe Timmy from down the street can do it."

That irritated Candy.

She was about to say, 'What am I, chopped liver?' when the TV blared to life. A Santa look alike laughed while a young girl danced her way through a tree lot while talking about the magic of Christmas. Candy felt some sympathy for the mom who appeared around a pine, and pulled the girl into her arms while chiding her for running off. The older man chuckled and assured the mom that getting lost in the

64

magic of Christmas was as fine a place as any to be.

It was too much. Rather than berate the magic or wallow in thoughts of her less-than-ideal situation, Candy donned her hat and coat.

The garage shelves held boxes of the outside decorations. Candy guessed the lights would be there, too. Poking around, she found white icicle lights stuffed in a plastic bin. A staple gun and box of industrial-sized staples lay on top. With a six-foot ladder in one hand and the bucket of lights in the other, Candy made her way to the front of the house. By the time she found the outlet and started hanging the lights, the cold air had stiffened her fingers, making progress slow. She finished and walked to the front to check her work.

"Hey, Candy!"

She whirled around, startled by the voice, but relieved to find it was just the teenage boy who lived on the other side of her. "Oh, hey, Timmy."

"Looks great," he said pointing to the lights.

"Thanks." She surveyed the lights making sure every one worked and didn't need any adjustment.

"You look great too." He waggled his eyebrows at her. "You should have called me, I would have held the ladder for you."

She laughed. "I managed just fine." She headed back toward Edie's house.

"Yeah. You did," he called. "But anyway, I'm selling fundraiser cards. You or Miss Marlowe want one?"

"Probably not."

"I'll bring them by later so you can see what's on them."

Candy flashed a thumbs-up to Timmy and slipped through the door. She hoped he wouldn't come back with useless fundraiser cards. The TV played a commercial of a snowman holding a diamond ring while a couple got engaged. It sent a spear of pain through her. She blinked back the tears that unexpectedly blurred her vision. The kitchen became her refuge until the ad ended.

"The lights are up, I'm going to go home now," she said hating the waver in her voice.

"Thank you." Edie turned to her. "What's wrong, dear? Did something happen outside?"

"No, nothing, I'm fine. Just, you know, commercials sometimes get to me." She hadn't talked about her broken engagement to anyone. And she wasn't about to start now.

Edie's expression softened as she turned the TV's volume down. "Christmas is a nice time to get engaged isn't it?"

Candy was horrified. Sure, it was a great time to get engaged, but what had been happy moments for her had turned out to be part of Andrew's 'next big thing.' Those memories got shoved back into a neatly wrapped package in her head before they even had a chance to escape the box.

With forced cheerfulness, Candy asked, "So, did you get engaged at Christmastime?"

"Oh, yes, dear. My Henry, he was a romantic." The faraway expression almost made Edie look young again. "Such a lovely evening we'd had. After dinner, he took me on a sleigh ride around the park. I remember, it was so cold." She rubbed her arms as if reliving the night. Then she chuckled. "But we were bundled up nice and warm under the blankets." She winked at Candy.

Surprised by the action, all Candy said was, "That sounds so nice." It did sound nice, but the thought also created a little ache in Candy's heart.

"It was. We stopped, right in front of the town Christmas tree. He helped me out and," she held out her hand, so Candy put hers in it. "And, he knelt, right there in the snow, in front of that beautiful sparkling tree and asked me." She sighed again then turned a serious look to Candy. "What about you, dear?"

Candy's mouth dropped open. Edie hadn't missed a thing. Her fingers tightened around Candy's hand almost imperceptibly as she started interrogating like she'd been a former KGB agent. Candy stoically gave the briefest of details, determined not to break down in front of Edie.

"That must have been very difficult," Edie said, releasing her hand and patting the couch. "Come, sit with me."

Emotionally drained, Candy obliged. Edie put her arm around Candy's shoulders and drew her close.

"Life is full of sorrows and heartbreaks. We all have them. Anyone who doesn't, hasn't lived yet." A tear trickled down Candy's cheek as Edie continued with a quiet sigh, "I miss my Henry every day, but we have to remember life is also full of joy and good people."

"Like you," Candy whispered.

"Like you." Edie's gentleness and the conviction in her tone brought more tears, but Candy fought to keep most of them at bay. Edie stroked Candy's hair. "Let it go, dear. Let it all out. Holding it in only makes it more painful."

Candy didn't relish the thought of having a breakdown right here on Edie's couch, but once the tears started in earnest, they were difficult to stop. Edie just held her and patted her shoulder occasionally, like the mom that had been absent so much of Candy's life.

She finally pulled herself together. The Hallmark Channel had been through several commercials and now returned to the movie.

"I'll let you get back to your show. I'm sorry about all the crying."

"Don't be, dear. I'm always here if you need to talk."

"Thank you. Is there anything else you need tonight?"

67

Edie shook her head, assessing Candy through slightly narrowed eyes. "What about you?"

"I'm good, now. I'll check in with you tomorrow," Candy said, waving as she ducked out the door before the movie evoked more yearning for love lost. The last thing she needed was to let Andrew back into her life just to dispel the loneliness.

The snow had stopped falling, but the temperature hadn't gotten the memo. The brisk wind stung Candy's bare face and hands. She jogged to her home next door, fumbling with the nativity box and her keys as she tried too quickly to open the front door. It wasn't much warmer inside. She dropped her keys on the table by the door and let the stillness surrounded her. Usually it was comforting after a hectic day, but tonight a disquiet filtered through the room.

The gas fireplace flickered to life when she flipped the switch, but it brought no comfort. She turned the lights on to dispel the gloom, but it followed her into the kitchen.

After putting the kettle on and putting tea leaves in her diffuser, she sorted through the mail, ignoring the solitude that weighed the air. A postcard from a local church with a nativity on the front invited the community to the Christmas Eve celebration. What was it today with the nativities?

She stared at the box on her counter. Packing tape held together the tattered corners. The picture showed wood figurines and words touted 'hand-carved Holy Land olive wood'. It wasn't a tiny set, or one with a few pieces. It was a serious collector's set. She set the mail on top of it blocking the beckoning faces.

The kettle whistled. The hot water over the diffuser sent a fragrant steam into the cool air. While the routine was comforting, the feeling that she'd neglected to do something nagged at her conscience. She needed to set up the nativity.

The emotions of the day pressed on her and she walked away, leaving the box on the counter. She just wanted to pretend Christmas was over already.

While busying herself with laundry and wiping down already clean counters, Candy kept pushing thoughts of the nativity away. But Edie wouldn't let it go until she admitted it was set up. Candy stifled a sigh and stood up straighter. Fine. The nativity would have its place, but it wouldn't change anything.

By the time she finished arranging the pieces on the sofa's end table, she was ready for that cup of chamomile tea and maybe streaming something from a cooking channel.

Candy wrapped her hands around the hot mug, savoring the warmth and the comforting scent of her nighttime ritual. Contestants on the cooking channel scurried around, making festive fare. This admittedly remained an enjoyable part of Christmas. She set the mug on the coffee table and pulled the chenille throw from the back of the couch. It caught on the Christ-child figurine.

Candy carefully detached the finely crafted piece from the blanket. The hay beneath baby Jesus had many tiny grooves and the detailed swaddling resembled a photo. She ran her finger over the smooth beams of the manger. Each one was unique and beautiful.

Like people. Yes, she thought, *like people.*

Tucking the soft folds of the blanket behind her, Candy sank into the comfort of the couch, still holding the olive wood piece. She should put it back, but languid as she felt, she simply closed her eyes while the contestants busily whipped up their desserts. In just a moment, she would return it to the empty spot between Mary and Joseph. The whirring and chopping and shouting lulled her as it faded into the night.

***

Candy stood in a semi-dark street. Ancient lamps hanging outside several doorways lit the cobblestones. People wearing colorful robes bustled in all directions. Many had a cloth covering their heads tied in place with cord. Some led animals through the streets, some called to each other in a language she didn't understand. None of them paid any attention to her.

A small boy with smudges on his face noticed her. He didn't say anything, just took her hand and pulled her toward a side street. At first she resisted. The boy looked up with his dark eyes full of questions. Panic evoked by an unfamiliar place should be crippling her by now, but instead, as he smiled, anticipation filled her. Something exciting lay ahead, something wonderful. They moved in tandem between the people and animals dotting the narrow streets.

The commotion grew distant as they journeyed along. The stars bathed the wide path in a soft light. Stone buildings, like sentinels, lined the path. As the boy led on, the houses grew farther apart. They walked for a few minutes, dust rising with each footstep until someone called to them from a distance. The boy didn't release her hand as he dodged a couple in the path, but instead hurried forward. The musty smell grew stronger and reminded Candy of the barn where her grandfather had kept his horses.

A hush enveloped them as soon as they stepped within the low walls surrounding the house. Shadows of tents and people dotted the large area outside. A woman held the curtain and motioned for them to come inside. She shooed the boy up the carved steps, leaving Candy without her guide.

The small amount of lamplight left the large room engulfed in shadows. Bedrolls littered the floor along the wall. A handful of ewes and their lambs had been corralled in one corner, where they appeared content and sleeping except for an occasional bleat. In the far corner across from the sheep, in what appeared to be another area to keep animals, a small group of people huddled together. The woman gestured toward them. Candy tiptoed through the maze of slumbering figures on the floor.

As she got closer, a feeling of peace and warmth flooded through her. A man drew her into the circle, his touch comforting and gentle. A woman sat on a mat looking exhausted, but somehow euphoric. A swaddled infant nestled into the crook of her arm. She gazed up at Candy, smiling and speaking words Candy didn't know but somehow understood to mean, "You're here."

Emotion choked her words so she just nodded. Yes, she was here. Here for this one moment that was more important than any other up to this time in history. God's son was born. She had not witnessed his birth as the ancient midwives in the house had and no words persuaded her. The scene spoke to her heart. To her soul. To her entire being. And she would forever be a witness that he had been born.

Mary's gaze dropped back to the baby. The love between them was overwhelmingly evident to Candy; it permeated the air and melted the ice around her heart. It dropped her to her knees. Mary reached over and took Candy's hand. The gesture brought tears that coursed down her face, though she struggled to stop them.

"Would you like to hold him?" Mary asked.

Again, no words would come, just a nod. Mary tenderly laid the babe in Candy's arms. Love beyond the depths she'd ever known, flowed through her. She soaked it up, amazed by the tiny being curled against her. If everyone could feel this, wouldn't they be kinder, more selfless? Wouldn't the world be a better place?

A few of the women fussed around Mary, adjusting the bedding and bringing food. As soon as she had finished eating, Mary focused on the Christ-child in Candy's arms. Not quite ready to give him back, Candy hesitated, but then returned the baby to Mary. The glow of his love still surrounded her. She noticed that it encompassed the entire little group.

Coming up next to her, a man knelt, offering a sack to the holy family. Candy's heart dropped as they thanked him. She had nothing to offer, had brought no gift. Mary, seeming to sense her distress, gestured to her backpack. Oh, no. Not that. Normally, it would carry her school stuff and laptop, but tonight, the only things in it were her sorrows and troubles.

Mary nodded, a tired smile offering encouragement. But it didn't seem fair to give those things. Besides, it was all she had right now so she clung to it. When she did, the quiet scene before her shifted and faded. She grabbed at the straw near her knees, but came away with air and a painfully poke into her palm.

Checking her hand, she saw the nativity piece gripped tightly. The living room came into focus as the red team on TV won the cooking challenge. Grabbing the remote, she clicked the TV off. Fire crackled through the logs in the gas fireplace. Everything was normal. Except her. She closed her eyes and replayed the vision she'd had still feeling the light within her.

A knock on the door blew through her peace. Frustrated by the interruption, she contemplated not answering, but found herself getting up instead.

72

"Hi Candy," said Timmy. "Whoa, you're glowing." He looked her up and down then nodded his head. "Weird. But I like it." He leaned toward her.

Glowing? Nonsense. Like his constant comments. Stupid high school boy.

"The answer is…"

He held up his hand, "I know, I know." He mimicked a female voice and said, "The answer is 'No, Timmy'." He put a hand on his hip, rolled his eyes, and continued in a passable mimicry, "'I am six years older than you and even if I weren't, I'm just not your type.'" He turned serious for a moment. "One of these days, you'll get tired of being alone and I'll be next door. At least for another year." He grinned at her. "Anyway, I brought the coupon cards for the basketball team fundraiser. How many do ya wanna buy?"

"Uh, none. Thanks." The light had faded--she'd felt it wane as she'd dismissed him. She didn't know how to get it back and wanted to yell at him for driving it away. In her gut, she knew she had driven it away herself with her irritation.

When she tried to shut the door he said, "Ah, c'mon. Why d'ya have to be such a Grinch?" He turned away, mumbling, "I only need to sell one more."

What was one more? He could be out selling for another hour. Or she could buy one and he could go home to his family—where he belonged, where his Italian mama would wrap him in a big hug and he would feel a bit of what she'd experienced tonight.

"Wait." she called to him out the door. "I'll buy one."

He turned on the sidewalk, but didn't move back towards the house. "Really?"

"Really, really." The wind picked up, biting at her face and the fingers she'd wrapped around the door frame. "Just come in. It's too cold out here."

She closed the door and went to get her purse from the kitchen. True to her instructions he let himself in.

"How much are they?" she asked, digging through her wallet.

"Twenty."

There went her lunch money for the week.

He walked over to the nativity. "This is cool," he said with awe in his voice.

"It's Mrs. Marlowe's." Candy couldn't help the protectiveness that surged through her. Or the defensiveness that she wouldn't be 'decking the halls.' "Besides the tree, it's my only decoration this year." Why was she telling him this? Like he cared?

Timmy looked from the nativity to Candy. "It's the only one that really matters."

Surprised at the mature answer, Candy nodded and held out the money. "Here you go."

"Although, on second thought, you could use some mistletoe."

"You wish, Timmy. You wish."

"That I do." He winked. "Another time, then."

She shook her head. "Never."

"Grinch."

"That only works once."

"Worth a try."

She laughed. The lightness, but a tiny speck inside her, glowed just a little.

Chapter 8

Jace arrived at Raxoco Resort's administrative offices on Thursday morning, a pit of dread heavy in his stomach. He sat in the reception area leafing through a news journal. The words and pictures blurred together, all his thoughts were distracted by the meeting ahead.

After he had flipped through several of the available magazines, a man approached looking like he'd walked right out of one. His shoes clicked against the stone floor. The shine on those shoes rivaled the ceiling's antique mirrored tiles. The impeccable ensemble included a jacket, vest and power tie. He seemed to size Jace up, but the effect was so subtle that Jace couldn't be sure.

"Mr. Marlowe?"

"Yes."

With the unease regarding Liesl's overly-friendly manner, Jace was grateful for the more formal greeting. He stood and extended his hand in greeting.

"Nice to meet you. I'm Andrew."

Jace nodded. "Nice to meet you, Andrew."

This was nothing more than small talk, but Jace was grateful for it. His nerves hummed like a hard drive low on memory.

"If you'll follow me."

Andrew led him to a small conference room smelling strongly of coffee.

"I'll let Ms. Thomas and Mr. Grayden know you're here. Help yourself," he said, his manner cool as he gestured toward a table.

Coffee urns and juice carafes accompanied by the necessary accoutrements occupied one side. Platters of pastries and colorful fruit sat on the other.

Jace's mouth watered as he selected a cheese Danish and poured a steaming cup of fresh coffee. The cream swirled light against the black in a marble circle. A bit of sugar and it was perfect. The pastry he'd selected disappeared quickly, but he savored the hot liquid sip by sip. He'd finished off a honey croissant just before a woman entered the room.

He stood, acknowledging her.

She strode over to him and held out her arms. He assumed it was Liesl and clearly, she was not expecting a handshake. Jace leaned down, giving her a hug, but taking care that only their shoulders touched.

"Welcome to the team," she said. "I'm Liesl."

"Nice to meet you," he replied.

Unlike Andrew, she wasn't quite what he expected. Someone like Liz would not have surprised him and the perfectly coifed hair and long manicured nails were spot on. But this fifty-something immaculately dressed woman who barely reached his shoulder, even in her stiletto heels, was not what he had imagined.

As she moved near, he pulled out a chair for her and then one for himself, which he immediately occupied.

He swiveled to face her. "Will Mr. Grayden be here soon? I'd like to get started."

"Something came up." Liesl shook her head. "He won't be able to meet with us today. But this isn't anything you and I can't take care of."

She smiled and, undeterred by his measures to avoid her, she pulled her chair as close as she could. They began reviewing the contract. She practically purred her words and occasionally stroked his arm. A bead of sweat tickled down his back. This interview could not end soon enough. After two hours of negotiation and dodging innuendos, the contract seemed satisfactory, but a small part of him still didn't trust her.

"This looks excellent, I'll take it home for another review and if everything is good, I'll send the signed copy back via e-mail."

She reached up and it took every bit of control for Jace not to flinch as her nails brushed against his hair.

"What other questions do you have?" The throaty tone repulsed him, but he had to get through this without offending her if he wanted to keep this gig.

"I just want to make sure we've covered everything, that's all."

"I like a man who covers all his bases." She looked through her too-long-to-be-real lashes. Her fingers caressed their way down his neck and bicep. "I'll meet you at Plaid Tycoon at 7:30 tonight and we can go over any other questions," she cooed.

The coffee and pastries soured in his stomach. He forced the feeling away and agreed to the meeting. It went against all his common sense but he needed an escape and figured this was the quickest way to get out. Besides, if he could get his sister, Katlyn, to go with him tonight, then maybe it wouldn't be so bad. It wouldn't make Liesl happy, but it would be better than confronting the precarious situation alone.

As he walked through the parking lot to his car, he called Kat. She already had plans for the night, but recommended a friend from college whose roommate worked at Plaid Tycoon. A few minutes of phone calls later, it was all worked out.

After arriving home, he combed through the contract. The only thing that concerned him was a line about being available to consult with the Director of Marketing at any of the resort's locations with expenses paid by the resort, plus a consultation fee. He made some adjustments and printed a new copy.

***

Night came sooner than Jace wanted, but he'd already played his ditch-the-boss card once and didn't trust it to work a second time. Besides, an unsigned contract was as good as no contract.

Kat had said Erin was a stickler for punctuality, so he arrived at her apartment a few minutes early. She flashed him a smile as she pulled on her coat. Jace noted the leather pants and cashmere sweater—very posh, very Liz. Panic rose within him but he took a deep breath. Katlyn would never set him up with someone like Liz. Still, doubts nagged at him, like why hadn't Kat tried to set them up before? Not that he was looking to date right now.

On the way to Plaid Tycoon, Erin talked about herself. A lot. Her job and the guys there who were always trying to find ways to date her, but she had a policy not to date guys from work. Her family, doting on her because she was the prettiest. College escapades, each not so subtly hinting at her popularity or her looks. It didn't take long to understand Katlyn's hesitation in setting them up. Just after 7:15, he and Erin walked into Plaid Tycoon.

The industrial style of Plaid Tycoon was a stark contrast to its name. The cool, sleek interior contained not one square of plaid aside from the logo. Concrete walls on both sides of the entry housed long gas fireplaces, running nearly the full length of the partition. Low flames licked artfully through glass rocks, dancing to the beat of a live band. Steel benches loaded with waiting people accompanied the welcome warmth.

Erin's roommate, working as the hostess, had a table ready for them. Jace noticed as they walked that Erin turned heads. Not that he blamed them. She was a looker. But so was Liz.

Once they got to the booth, Erin informed her friend they were waiting for one more and gave her Liesl's name. Jace slid beside her on the bench tucking his briefcase behind his legs.

They sat for a few moments, perusing the menu. When the waiter came, Erin ordered a margarita. Jace ordered water. Erin shot him a look and ordered another drink.

"You might need it," she said to Jace.

Less than ten minutes from the time they'd sat down, Liesl slid into the booth across from them, a cold smile creasing the heavy makeup.

"Jace." Her lip twitched as if holding back a sneer. "I didn't realize you were bringing someone."

"Ms. Thomas, this is Erin, Erin, Ms. Thomas."

Erin held out her hand and Liesl shook it, quickly letting go to flag down the waiter. After ordering a martini and some appetizers, she looked at Jace, completely ignoring Erin.

"I'm sure you found everything to your satisfaction."

Jace retrieved the contract from his bag.

"There is only one thing," he said pointing to the highlighted phrase about his availability to consult.

She skimmed over it then waved him off as she said, "That's in all the contracts, but you know we'll only be working on the Saint Angelo location."

"I revised that, so it is specific to the Saint Angelo location and that consultations are limited to one time per month. The consultation fee is twice my normal hourly rate." He paused as her lips tightened into a line, but he didn't want any part of consulting to be directly with her, so he put the updated contract on top of the old one and forged on. "This draft includes the changes. I'm sure you'll want to go over it, but I've signed it, so if you're okay with the amendments, it just needs your signature."

She tapped her manicured nail on the paper while scanning it. "Of course I will look over it." She tucked it into her purse as the appetizers and her martini arrived.

As she sipped, Jace wondered what schemes she toyed with in her head. He would have to be on constant guard. Certainly she wouldn't forgive or forget that he'd thwarted whatever she'd had in mind for tonight. Or was he just being conceited? After nibbling on a few celery sticks, Liesl pulled a fifty-dollar bill from her wallet and left it on the table.

"Enjoy the rest of your evening," she said without looking at them and then walked away, softly dragging her nails along his arm as she left.

Jace fought the revulsion. Why did this job feel like his only option besides being homeless?

Erin chuckled, bringing him back around. "Wow. She has it bad."

"Has what bad?"

"Cougar girl clearly wants you for her boy-toy." Erin sized him up. "Can't say that'd be a bad thing. You could be my boy-toy."

Jace was horrified. "Never been the kind of guy for a fling. Even a convenient one."

"Too bad. You're missing out." She sipped her margarita, her eyes laughing at him over the salted rim.

He moved to sit across from her and ordered more appetizers. He stayed away from the extra margarita she'd ordered for him. He needed a clear head.

Not much later, he walked her to her apartment door. She

backed up against it in what he assumed she thought was an enticing pose.

"Aren't you going to kiss me good-night?"

He leaned in and pecked her on the cheek, hoping she wouldn't turn and try to make out with him.

"Really? That's all I get? C'mon, I did you a huge favor tonight."

And for that he was grateful, but the kiss would mean nothing and he didn't operate that way.

"You're right." He paused. When she looked hopeful he said, "I have a solution. His name is Ladd. I think you'd get along well with him. He lives about ten minutes from here. I'll call him and introduce you."

She scowled. "Ugh. I don't want a guy who can't get his own dates."

He dialed Ladd's number anyway and said to Erin, "You went out with me."

"True. Because your sister asked me to." She smirked. "And she promised me you were hot."

Ladd answered, saving him from having to respond to her suggestive comment. He held up a finger while talking to Ladd, who agreed to come by saying he'd just left a bar a few miles away.

After hanging up, Jace said, "You want something. I'm going to deliver, just not the way you expected. And I think you'll find it a much better fit."

Erin folded her arms across her chest but didn't say anything. Great. Why did dating have to be this way? Not that he considered this a date.

"Listen," he said breaking the silence. "You have no idea how much I appreciate you going along with me tonight." He rubbed the back of his neck. "That woman scares me."

That elicited a giggle.

"She should." Erin grinned then shrugged. "I suppose you could call me again if she persists." Erin pulled her coat tighter. "Why are we standing out here? We can wait inside. I promise not to bite."

"Sure."

She handed him her key. He hesitated, then took it, praying Ladd wouldn't be long. Five minutes of listening to Erin talk about her college days seemed an eternity. Ladd showed up as she finished a crash-the-frat-party story. A few introductions later, Jace left them chatting on the couch in Erin's apartment.

Jumping in his car he cranked the volume of the radio to stave off the exhaustion that surrounded him. When he arrived home he fell onto his bed and didn't wake until morning.

***

It took until the afternoon to complete contract negotiations with Raxoco. On the final call, Liesl had purred through the phone about the upcoming trip to Saint Angelo and the time they would have to 'get to know each other'. It made his skin crawl but thankfully, his job shouldn't require a lot of personal interaction between them. And Andrew would be there, so Jace hoped he would act as a buffer.

Andrew had also contacted him with detailed information for the hotel and transportation. Jace had considered requesting tickets to the Chorale, but ultimately hadn't had the courage. He would work something out when he got to St. A, even if it meant waiting in the parking lot.

He had also declined company transportation, saying he would drive himself since he planned to go over sooner than Liesl and Andrew. That had seemed to cheer Andrew up.

Weird.

Jace settled in to work on updating the code and layout of the pet shelter website. In the middle of revamping some menu options, a knock on the door pulled him from his work. He opened it to find Earl, the apartment manager and the stench of stale smoke.

"Yeah. Marlowe. We're one week into December and I ain't seen your rent yet." He pulled a cigarette from the package in his shirt pocket. "No cash in hand by five o'clock tonight, I'll be slapping an eviction notice on your door." Earl flicked his lighter and took a long drag. "Don't care that it's December." Smoke ghosted around his mouth and then he blew the rest at Jace.

Jace coughed, waving the smoke away.

"What are you talking about?"

"December? Christmas? I don't want to be a Scrooge, but …"

Another draw on the cigarette interrupted the end of Earl's sentence. Jace glared at Earl. He didn't know what this was about, but he did know the rent had been paid.

"I paid the rent last Saturday. Put it in the After Hours drop," he said, hating the tension in his voice. How could this be happening?

"Like I said, I ain't seen it." Earl pointed the cigarette at Jace and said, "You're a chump, Marlowe and I've given you a lotta breaks. But this time I'm done. If you can't afford to live here, it's time to move on."

Jace held up his hand. "Please go look again. I paid it last week." He shoved the full-blown panic deep in his gut. No way would he let Earl in on that secret.

Blowing smoke toward the eaves, Earl shook his head and said, "Owner don't like sketchy tenants. I keep making excuses, but I ain't covering for you this time."

Sketchy tenants? What about sketchy landlords? He'd been so happy to have the funds to pay rent that he hadn't considered that paying cash, after hours, maybe wasn't the best idea. Now, it looked like he was out a lot of rent and an expensive place to live. Losing the high-end apartment wouldn't be a bad thing, except he'd paid the rent.

"Listen, Earl. I paid it last Saturday. In the After Hours drop. Maybe it's still there."

"It ain't. I check the box daily."

Jace made a mental effort to slow his breathing, searching for a solution. "Maybe it got stuck inside?"

"Maybe you just didn't pay it." Earl sneered. "At any rate, it's gotta be paid. Five o'clock tonight or …" Earl drew his finger across his neck, then walked away.

Jace ran his fingers through his hair. Earlier today, he'd been grateful for the upfront payment from Raxoco that would cover the rest of December's expenses and pay off some debt. He'd thanked his Creator for this blessing. Now, as he stared at the ceiling, the weight of survival descended. He closed the door and dropped to his knees. The air around him too heavy to breathe. Leaning against the door, he prayed. His first real prayer in a long time.

St. A popped into his head. Going there with Raxoco would take care of one week. The week before Christmas. Maybe he could crash at Kat's after that, until he found another place. Ski slopes and two-way streets interrupted his thoughts but he pushed them away. Sure, the best skiing was in St. A but it came with a price tag not in his budget. It was also not a reason to go back or to stay.

What he would not do is call his parents or stay with his grandma. Warm memories flooded his mind—running through her backyard in the summer, building snow forts with Grandpa Henry, laughing till his cheeks hurt. But those days would never come back. At least Raxoco would give him a reason to be there and a reason to split. If he stayed with Grandma, she wouldn't want him to go and Jace knew all-too-well the guilt she could readily wield.

His dad, on the other hand, would require double shifts on the building sites. Jace was in great physical shape and knew the trade, so the demands of construction didn't concern him. It was the constant expectation of 'more' and 'better' that left him empty.

His dad had always assigned him to the teams managing the early stages of construction. It wasn't until college he discovered the satisfaction of a finished project. Especially one that was both functional and aesthetic. It's what drove him in every job he took now. Working for his dad again, the barely-begun structures would provide no fulfillment and there would be no time for job-hunting or work on his own ventures.

Running both hands over his unshaven face, he inhaled deeply and slowly. All he could do was go forward and focus all his efforts on updating the pet place and children's museum websites. Wait for the eviction notice. Pack up and find a new place to live. Survive.

At five o'clock, Jace heard a scuffle outside his door. It took a few minutes for him to move. He checked the peephole, but it had been covered. As he opened the door, a cold blast of wind stole his breath. True to his word, Earl had pasted an eviction notice on the door. Jace yanked down the sign. He scrawled, *Paid in Full* across the page. It was a true statement.

He wanted to crumple the paper, wanted to throw it in Earl's face. His fist tightened around the edge of the paper. He had caught a break and suddenly, his rent disappeared? How could Earl do this? He was, as usual, a class act.

85

Without even putting a jacket on, Jace traipsed down to the office and slid the now folded paper in the After Hours drop, not caring about the cold or the wet snow collecting on his shirt.

Over most of the next week, Jace waited, unsuccessfully, for a response from Earl. In the meantime, he'd completed half the updates to the museum's home page and a few for the pet shelter. With that on the back burner, he printed a copy of the specs for Raxoco and laid them on the kitchen counter. He scribbled a few notes as he reviewed their requests. Ideas flowed as he contemplated how to create a page that would exceed their expectations and yet allow visitors to easily navigate through the site.

A visit to the actual location would almost certainly give him the rest of the information he needed. He planned to pack his car and leave tomorrow evening, stay in a hotel near the church, and show up for his grandma's performance on Saturday night. Maybe they would have some stand-by tickets or maybe he could hang out in the foyer. Excitement over surprising Grandma Edie drowned out the apprehension of going back to St. A, and more amazingly, the dread of working closely with Liesl and Andrew for a whole week.

Chapter 9

A layer of snow had covered Candy's car by the time her shift at the care center ended. Quickly brushing it off the windows, she shook the still-falling snow from her hair and coat, and jumped into her car. After a call to Edie, Candy pulled onto the snow-packed streets. The falling flakes grew in size as she made her way across town flipping through her favorite stations as she went.

A forecaster's voice boomed over the radio's airwaves. "…Severe weather system heading our way late this evening and through tomorrow night." Had he even looked outside? "This storm system looks like it could blanket outlying areas in several feet of snow tonight. Shepherd's Pass will require chains if you're heading in or out of Saint Angelo. If you don't have to travel, I'd recommend staying inside. The high will be twenty-nine and the low seventeen. A cold front is right behind this storm and temperatures will be dropping Sunday with record lows possible. Stay toasty, folks."

Candy turned off the radio and let the sounds of the slush and rush of commuters surround her. A few people had slid around the corner in front of her, so she let off the gas and eased into the turn. The SUV was a wonder in the snow, which had been her second-biggest reason for buying it. The first had to do with Andrew, so she pushed that memory away. After a thirty-minutes-longer-than-usual commute, she pulled into her garage.

Dodging the barrage of flakes, Candy ran to the mailbox and grabbed a lone letter before hurrying inside. Warm air welcomed her like an old friend who was always at the ready with a big hug. The lamp cast its usual glow as she went through her habit of dropping her keys and opening the mail on her way to the kitchen.

Rummaging through the sparse contents of the refrigerator, Candy pulled out some vegetables. Roasted chicken, in Edie's fridge from last night's meal, would provide some protein. She buttoned her coat and hesitated on the doorstep. A curtain of falling snow nearly hid Edie's house. Pulling up her collar, Candy jogged through the storm. She shook out her hair and coat and walked in.

Edie looked up from her easy chair. "There you are, dear." She stared past Candy. "Oh, my, looks like Mother Nature is serious tonight."

Candy laughed as she shut the door. "I guess that's one way of looking at it. I thought we could have soup tonight."

"Sounds yumm-o. How can I help?"

It was a different variation of the same conversation every night. Their comfortable routine followed. They would talk about their day while Candy made dinner and Edie went through her exercises.

After eating, Candy would clean up and make some snacks and sandwiches for Edie to eat during the day. She knew from experience that Edie would do it on her own, probably with the fracture boot off. It eased Candy's mind to leave things that were easy for Edie to do and wouldn't require a lot of standing. Typically she would then return home to schoolwork or a project. Although finals were over, she had the last of the preparations for the Christmas Chorale to go over. It was important to her that everything be perfect.

Back at her house, she went through her checklist, twice. Everything looked in order and she still had time before bed. She set the planning notebook on the counter next to her handbag and a couple of books her friend Allie had said she "must read." Maybe she could relax with the one she hadn't started.

The first one she'd abandoned four chapters in. The main character had been left at the alter while her fiancé had run off with a bridesmaid. A story too like her own to continue reading. She had intended to return the book, but through self-torture or forgetfulness—she hadn't decided which—it still lay on her counter.

She tucked the other book under her arm and headed to the couch. Instead of diving right in, she watched a renovation show. Someday, it would be fun to do some renovations. But first, she needed to graduate, get a better paying job, and buy her own place. Another episode started, drawing her in. When it ended, she turned it off realizing if she didn't, it would soon become a marathon. Picking up the book, she snuggled deeper into the corner of the couch.

The gray-blue afghan her grandmother had crocheted for her never failed to bring out the longing for home, but she wasn't ready to face that yet. Opening the pages, she released a sigh and started Chapter One. After re-reading that same paragraph several times, she gave up and maneuvered the book between the camel and the manger of the nativity set, pushing them back a bit. This offset the shepherd so he was staring in the opposite direction from the group.

Candy picked him up.

"Doesn't do any good to have you looking away from the Light of the World. Darkness will never be your friend."

He didn't reply, but it seemed to her that if he could, he would agree. How long had she been turned away from the Light? Too long.

She cradled the figurine in her hands, studying the fine details. The grain of the wood followed the outline of the shepherd's cloak, as if the wood and the carver had worked in unison to create the illusion. A knot in the crook of his arm had been masterfully transformed into a lamb.

89

Candy glanced at the other pieces, but knowing they would have the same attention to detail, she continued to examine the shepherd. The staff, half-hidden in his robes, curved up and around, ensuring that no sheep would be lost. How nice it would be to have someone look after you and care for you in the way the shepherd cared for his flock. The symbolism went straight to her heart. Christ was the great Shepherd and He cared for her. Perhaps this was His way of reaching out and bringing her back in. The lines blurred and she leaned her head back and closed her eyes.

Would he reach for the backpack full of her sorrows and fears? Did she have the courage—or even the power—to surrender that burden? The answer frightened her. No peace would come until she gave it over to Him, yet she clung to it like a child would her favorite toy. Sleep beckoned, promising a reprieve from the weight of her worries.

***

The driver of the car gripped the wheel with gloved hands, leaning forward slightly in his seat. His chiseled jaw had the barest hint of a shadow. Dark waves of hair reached his collar, tousled but not unruly. If he were a character in the book Allie wanted her to read, Candy was certain it would describe him as "devastatingly handsome." Not that she would argue.

Candy pulled her gaze away. No radio played, but the time showed 1:17 a.m. They drove down Shepherd's Pass through an intense storm. The sign declaring 'Saint Angelo, Population 7,531, 5 Miles Ahead' appeared, but only the word 'Angel' showed through the snow stuck to it. They sped toward the curve locals jokingly called Shepherd's Hook.

"Slow down," Candy said gripping the dash. But the driver gave her no heed. Rather, he leaned forward even more. "There's a curve." The panic in her voice had no effect, except to tighten the knot in her stomach. "Slow down!"

He let his foot ease off the gas and the car slowed, but it was too late. Halfway through the curve the car spun. Candy heard someone screaming. She clamped her mouth shut when she realized the sound was her own. Like a bad ride at the State Fair, the car completed another spin, hit the edge of the road and flipped onto the driver's side. Candy hung in the air, held in place by her seatbelt. She took a deep breath and checked on the driver whose body now rested against the door.

"What in the world?" he said struggling to right himself.

"You were going too fast." Candy didn't want to argue, didn't want to accuse, but he should have listened. "Are you all right?"

He huffed out a breath. "Guess I'm not going much farther like this." He released his seatbelt.

"Be careful. Wait. What are you doing?"

He pushed the button on the door and the window rolled down. Icy air from the packed snow rushed into the car. Candy shivered, pulling her sweater tighter around her and tucking it close against her body, where the belt would allow. Why didn't she have a coat?

The stranger maneuvered so that his feet were planted in the window space. In one smooth heft, he pushed the car upright and was left standing in the snow. The movement jostled Candy into her seat. She was again thankful for the seatbelt that restrained her.

The man got back in the car. Whatever cologne he wore swirled over her on the rush of icy air that entered the car with him. It went right along with Allie's novel. He smelled heavenly. But that meant nothing at this point because they were stuck five miles from town. Candy was familiar enough with winter travel to doubt that the car would be going anywhere, but maybe he would surprise her.

He put the car in gear and Candy heard the whine of the tires as they spun.

"Hold on, I'll get out and push," she said thinking he would offer to push instead while she drove.

He simply hit the steering wheel with the palm of his hand before gripping it again. "Unbelievable," he said, staring out at the flakes that had only gotten bigger. His lips tightened. After a moment he closed his eyes and leaned his forehead on his hands. "Dear God, I need help," he whispered into the silence of the car.

Candy wasn't God and she didn't know how to help. They could wait in the car for someone to come along, which was about as likely as getting struck by lightening tonight. They could walk, but she only had a sweater on and, although he probably had a coat in the back, he was only wearing a button-down shirt—no tie—and slacks.

The man picked up his phone then tossed it back on the middle console. "What good's the battery when I can't even get a signal?"

"It's the Pass. The signal's never good through here," she commented. He merely tapped at the wheel as if deciding what to do. "I'll push," she said, figuring that was a better option than walking.

She opened her door to a barrage of icy flakes determined to turn her into a giant snowball. Shaking them off, she turned to go to the back of the car. Her feet slipped. She tried to maintain her balance, but the ground met her bottom soundly.

With a jerk, Candy opened her eyes, expecting wet and cold, but found herself instead in the warmth of her living room. The shepherd lay in her lap. Confusion evaporated with the dream. Or had it been a vision? Replacing the figurine, she threw off the afghan and bolted into action. Thirty seconds later, a twin sized comforter tumbled in the dryer and chicken broth turned in the microwave. Armed with an extra pair of wool socks, the semi-heated comforter—but she couldn't wait any longer—and a thermos of hot broth, she waddled out to her garage.

The main roads through town weren't too bad. A plow had gone through not too long ago, but once she passed the town limits, they became more precarious and forced her to slow down. The wipers swished back and forth, pushing fluffy snowflakes from the windshield. She squinted into the night, much like she'd seen the driver of the car in her dream do. A few minutes of that and a dull ache formed at her temples. Where was Shepherd's Hook? It should be just ahead. Snow banks guided her and she was grateful that enough snow had fallen previously to build them up at the roadsides. Dim lights glowed up ahead and relief filled her. Not much farther to go.

The car was just like in her dream, off the road enough that it stuck in the bank. She flashed the high beams of her headlights and waited for the driver to get out. The night was quiet all around her. No movement aside from the giant swirling flakes. Candy peered through the storm but didn't see anyone. Getting out, she hurried to the other car. No one sat inside. Fresh footprints led away from the car. This could not be good.

"Hello?" she called into the night. "Hello!" This time, louder than before. Nothing.

Back in her car, with the heat on high and her window

93

cranked down, she crept along, following the footprints until they disappeared over the bank of the ravine. Her heart dropped. Worst-case scenarios started rolling through her mind. There was no way she could haul a body up the steep side even if it was only about ten feet down at any given spot. Quickly she rolled up her window. Opening her door she jumped out of the car and gingerly stepped through the inches of white fluff to the edge. A snow-covered creature rose from the gully. Startled, she stifled a scream and stumbled backward into the car. Relief filled her for the second time that night.

"Hey." She reached out and grabbed his elbow, pulling him the rest of the way up. "Are you all right?" she asked. Even under all that snow he was better in real life.

"I think so," he said pulling his arm away and shaking the snow from his jacket. "Took a tumble trying to get the attention of a passing car." He glared at her. "Probably you."

She stared in disbelief. "You're welcome." The sarcasm couldn't be stopped. "Maybe you'd like to stay out here all night?"

"No. I wouldn't," he snapped back.

"Great, then get in." Her tone wasn't any more cheerful than his.

One of his shoes sloshed as he walked away from her. He must've broken through the ice of the stream below. Images of her car smelling like swamp filled her head. "Wait." Candy grabbed a plastic trash bag from the back of her car. His pants were wet—well, had been, now they were wet *and* frozen. That would be another mess on the floor of her car. Not happening. "Put your pants and socks and shoes in here. I've got extra socks and a blanket you can wrap up in."

"You want me to take my pants off?"

"Yes." She paused. "Or I guess you could get in the bag.

He gave her a funny look as she handed him the bag.

"Sorry. I'm a little weird about my car. It's freezing out here, though, so let's get a move on."

Reaching into the back seat she grabbed the blanket. "Hurry up or this will all be covered with snow, too."

He shivered violently, dislodging a layer of snow, but then obliged and began struggling with the buckle of his belt.

After several attempts, she tossed the blanket on the seat and pushed his hands out of the way. "Let me, please, so we're not here all night." Unclasping the buckle with clinical precision born of working at the care center, she sat him in the car with his pants around his ankles.

"Judging by your ability, you must do that often." His tone held a bit of irritation and possibly criticism.

"Almost every day." And she laughed. "Mr. Charles gets a bit cranky if I take too long." The look on his face was priceless. "There's hot broth in the thermos if you want some," she said, changing the subject.

She tucked the blanket around him, but struggled a bit with the socks because her own fingers had begun to stiffen from the low temperatures.

"Do you always travel this prepared?"

"Nope." No point in explaining a story no one but the shepherd would believe. She shook the snow from her hair and coat and got in the car, welcoming the warmed seat and heat blowing over her. Whoever invented seat warmers was a genius.

"We have a couple of options," she said. "We can go back and I can try to pull your car out of the snow bank. We can also go back and get anything you left in the car that you may need. Or…" Staring into the storm, she put both hands on the wheel and stifled the smirk that threatened behind her seriousness. "Or, we can just head straight into town and you can get Darwin the tow-truck driver to pull you out tomorrow. I highly recommend him. He's very friendly."

What was wrong with her? She was accustomed to grumpy patients, but tonight it seemed this guy was getting to her.

"If it's not too much for you," he said, challenge lacing his words, "I need to at least get my briefcase and possibly my suitcases."

He glanced over at her, but she ignored him. With the Cherokee in gear, she flipped the car around to go back to his car. The silence between them grated on her, but she refused to break it. Besides, she needed all her concentration for the road. She didn't need the distraction of his tousled hair dripping onto the blanket or his five o'clock shadow or the way he smelled. Or his sarcasm, she reminded herself.

She pulled up next to his car. "Keys are in your pants pocket?"

"Yes. I'd get them but," he winked and a smile twitched the corner of his mouth, "the abominable snowman took my pants and shoes."

There was no response for that except her open mouth, which she promptly shut and got out to retrieve the keys from the back of the car. The blizzard swirled around her, blowing at the strands of hair sticking out from her cap. Flakes again melted on her cheeks. It didn't take her long to haul the briefcase from the front seat and two suitcases from the trunk.

When she climbed in the handsome stranger said, "Thank you." No sarcasm or arrogance this time, just gratitude.

A little confused by his sudden meekness, she said, "You're welcome." She sighed as she stared out into the reality of the snowstorm. "But maybe don't thank me yet-- we're still miles from the nearest house."

He chuckled. "Then maybe we should get going?"

"Yeah, sorry." The pounding in her head heightened as once again she concentrated on the blur in front of her. Staying on the road was paramount—obviously.

"Where were you headed tonight?" he asked.

Apparently, his attitude had thawed with the rest of him. How to answer that question? A half-smile battled with her self-control. The complete answer would remain her little secret. As for now, she would share only part of it. "Up the pass, but now I'm heading to wherever you're staying for the night." She hazarded an inquisitive glance in his direction.

"I was supposed to be staying at Fernwood Resort, near the church. But when I called to let them know I wouldn't arrive until late tonight, they said they had overbooked and didn't have a room." Staring ahead, he went on, "The roads were too bad to check the Internet, so I figured I'd find something once I arrived." He leaned his head back and closed his eyes. "I can start checking once I have service again."

She didn't stay in hotels and hadn't paid much attention to them. A couple of times a week, on her way to school, she passed the Belnap B&B. It sprawled across an acre of forest at the bottom of the Pass; however, it was probably closed for the night. The throbbing in her temples waned a little. She just wanted to be home in her warm bed. But what to do with the stranger next to her? It was a dilemma for sure. The image of him wrapped in a blanket missing half his clothes and trying to explain his situation to a hotel manager brought a low chuckle.

He turned to look at her saying, "Or, I guess I'm at your mercy?"

"Actually, you'd be at the mercy of the hotel's front desk."

He looked down, a half--smile spreading across his tired face. "I can dress in the unloading zone."

Candy full out laughed. It was too late and things that shouldn't be humorous, tickled her funny bone. "I'm sure that will go over well." She paused, losing sight for a moment of the tracks from her trip up. "Too bad Allie's not working tonight," she said under her breath.

She let off the gas. They were only going twenty miles per hour, but the storm had worsened, making it difficult to go even that fast. Panic knotted in her stomach until she spotted the tire marks again.

"Why?"

Had he said something? She'd lost track of the conversation. "Sorry. Why what?"

"You said it's too bad Allie isn't working. Why?"

"Oh, that. She works the desk at a hotel near the college and she probably could help you out." Allie was one of those girls everyone liked. She was always surrounded by her group of friends when Candy saw her at school. "Especially if she saw you dressing." Candy teased.

She watched for his reaction out of the corner of her eye and hated herself for judging him to be like Andrew.

He shook his head. "I guess I could try Hotel Lush and charge it to Raxoco, or maybe I'll just go to my grandma's." He pulled the blanket tighter. "I was supposed to surprise her tomorrow night, but I guess it'll just have to happen earlier than I planned."

This was a new angle and not what she expected. Something in what he'd said was important, but her tired brain couldn't pinpoint what it was.

She arched an eyebrow his direction and asked, "Where does she live? We can at least get you to a hotel close to her … after you put on some pants, of course." She giggled to herself again, but stopped short. Hotel. Raxoco. Her mind struggled a half second more. That was the company buying her school. This … this evil creature in her car was there to steal her dreams. He wasn't even paying attention to her; he scrolled through his phone instead.

"Her address is 2274 N. Harmony Avenue."

What? He repeated the address. Candy's heart nearly stopped. That was Edie's address. That meant this … this funny, handsome guy was actually *the* Jace Marlowe? She wanted to shake her fist at the Universe. God definitely had a sense of humor, but she didn't find this funny. At all. She tried to cheer herself up. Maybe this was a different grandson, one she didn't know about. But Edie only had one grandson—one perfect, beautiful grandson who, it appeared, worked for the company hatching evil plots to upend her world. Disbelief filled her. How could he be part of something that would take something so precious from his community?

Candy took a deep breath and said with forced cheer, "I know right where that is. I can take you that far."

He leaned back into the seat again. "Thank you."

Replays of the night ran through her head as she concentrated on the road. A few minutes later, a soft snore broke the silence. His features, relaxed in sleep, made him even more appealing. A wolf in sheep's clothing, she reminded herself, pulling her attention back to the road.

A tiny glow of one of the two stoplights in town cut through the night. Not too much farther and the streets should at least be discernible. And she could drive faster. And get this guy out of her car.

The plows had cleared and sanded the main roads, but hadn't made it to the Avenues yet. Candy slowed as she turned onto her street, but the car fishtailed anyway. Jace startled awake.

"Sorry," was all she said keeping her focus on the snow-covered lane.

"I'm the one who should apologize for falling asleep."

Yeah, he should apologize, for dragging her out in a blizzard in the middle of the night, for complicating her life, but not for sleeping.

"No need for that." She forced her hands to relax on the wheel. "We're almost there. Do you have a key?"

"No." His half smile held chagrin. "I actually haven't been here in a long time. And I planned to surprise her after the concert tomorrow, or I guess tonight." He looked out the window as the houses passed and sighed. "It was probably a stupid plan anyway. Maybe her door will be open and I can just be there when she gets up in the morning." He ran his fingers through his still-damp hair. "I couldn't get tickets and I don't even know where to buy flowers. I figured the hotel gift shop would have something."

"That's not a stupid plan."

She'd like to rearrange his other plans but right now she needed a strategy for dealing with this unexpected situation. She should have left him in that snowbank. Even as she thought it, she dismissed it for the nonsense it was. It wasn't who she was.

"I can help you," she said.

Edie would be over the moon.

"Her house is right there," he said pointing.

Candy hit the button to open her garage. Rather than stopping at Edie's, she drove up her driveway and out of the swirling flakes. Instead of getting out, she stared at the door that led into the house. What was she doing? Exhaustion had clearly fogged her reasoning. She took a deep breath.

He pointed towards Edie's then at Candy. "You're her

neighbor."

"Yes." She ignored the comment otherwise and said, "Here's what I think we should do." She couldn't look at him. Couldn't face Mr. Perfect. Partly because she saw him as the squasher of dreams, but also because looking at him stole her breath away. "You can crash on my couch. Tomorrow, I'll take you to Darwin's Towing. They can get your car. If you want to lie low, you can hang out here." She couldn't believe she even offered this. "I have a bunch of things to do for the Chorale, including picking up arrangements from the florist. Do you know what kind of flowers you want for Edie?" Every part of her ached from concentrating on the road home. She rolled her shoulders to ease the tension.

"You don't mind? I really hoped to surprise her. She likes carnations. Pink ones."

Candy nodded. Her insides twisted a little. He knew her favorite flower. He seemed a devoted grandson, so why had he stayed away so long?

"And if they don't have carnations?"

"She likes daisies, too. I think that's what they are. She always grew them by her front porch."

Candy nodded again.

"The concert part will be a little trickier. I have to be there at three o'clock. Edie isn't supposed to be there until four, but since I'm her ride, she's going at three." She tapped the wheel thinking of options. "It's fifteen minutes to the church, so going back and forth doesn't really make sense."

She finally looked his direction. And it happened again. Her breath vanished.

He regarded her with an intensity she wasn't accustomed to.

Her attention returned to the door. She had to think. But it was so late. Or early if she wanted to be technical.

"Actually, let's sleep on it. We can work out the details in the morning."

Candy went around back and popped open the hatch. Jace appeared with the blanket wrapped around his lower half. She reached in to get a suitcase and he put his hand on her arm. Even through the coat, his touch sent tingles like little ice fairies dancing up to her shoulder.

"I can get them."

Barely able to form a resistive thought, she simply bobbed her head in agreement. Then, as sort of an afterthought, she retrieved the bag of his wet clothes. He waited and followed her inside, managing the two suitcases and his briefcase like they weighed nothing. Which was completely contrary to her own experience with them.

Setting the bag on the kitchen floor, she pointed out the bathroom to him.

"I'll get you some blankets and a pillow," she said, all the while avoiding eye contact.

She was unsure how a person could undo her resolve with a look, but he could. Fatigue—and resentment she reminded herself—weighed heavy on her as she moved down the hall to gather some bedding. He followed with a suitcase, taking a detour at the washroom.

Candy hurried to tuck the sheet into the couch, hoping to be done and in her room before he returned. As she tossed the pillow at the end of the couch, he came into the hall wearing pajama pants. That was all. Blessed day that his suitcase bumped the wall and he didn't see her gaping.

Ducking down, she pretended to smooth the sheet. It didn't prevent the blush from flooding over her. She was helpless to stop it. You'd think she'd never seen a man before. Well, not often one that was that well put together.

She reminded herself that he was here with a company that planned to close the campus.

Candy inhaled deeply. It didn't matter that he had the power to crush her plans. It didn't matter that he was the finest thing in all of humanity. What mattered, she reminded herself, was Edie. This adversary would become a pawn in her plot to make this the best Christmas ever for her sweet neighbor. That's how she would have to look at it. Problem solved.

"There you go," she said gesturing to the couch. "Extra blankets if you need them." She pointed to a chair.

"Thank you."

Halfway down the hall already, she called back, "You're welcome. Good night."

For two seconds before she succumbed to sleep, she wondered what she would do if he weren't the enemy.

Chapter 10

Jace rolled over in the darkness. What a crazy night. But somehow it had all worked out. He'd ended up next door to Grandma Edie at the home of a very attractive lady. What if she had a boyfriend? Or a husband? Something about that unsettled him. On top of that, he didn't even know her name.

No way the beautiful woman could also be the practical, thoughtful neighbor who had spent the last few weeks caring for his grandma. And thank goodness for that, because Grandma Edie might start doing more than hint at getting them together. He drifted to sleep, wondering how he'd become so shallow.

Jace woke to soft clinking. It took a moment to realize he wasn't on his old mattress. Shifting on the couch, he saw the faint glow of light from the kitchen. He thought she'd gone to bed. His phone read 5:30. Those few hours had gone way too fast. It was Saturday morning. Shouldn't she be sleeping in?

As he swung his legs over the edge of the couch, the blanket fell away and cool air surrounded him. He shivered and reached for his suitcase. By the time he'd unzipped it and pulled on a shirt, she stood in the doorway.

"Sorry," she whispered. "I didn't mean to wake you. Go back to sleep, I'll be back after ten."

She disappeared into the kitchen. He followed. A cell phone on the counter illuminated the cabinets and cast shadows around the room. As he sat on a stool facing her, she glanced over.

"Sorry, I don't drink coffee. Would you like tea?"

"Sure."

She handed him the mug she'd already prepared and got a

thermos out of the cupboard. He wrapped his hands around the warm cup and savored the fragrant steam.

"I don't even know your name."

She hesitated then said, "Candy."

Jace raised his eyebrows. Her lips pressed together in a thin line but she didn't offer any other information. He sat unmoving, afraid to say or do the wrong thing. It was too early to decipher women.

"Usually I get some joke about it," she said regarding him intently. "Especially since my last name is Kaine."

He put the two together. "Your parents named you Candy Cane?"

She shook her head. "It's actually K-a-i-n-e, and my mother named me Candice."

Warning bells went off in Jace's head and he struggled to find the reason. Candy interrupted his thoughts.

"My father, who never bothered to marry my mother, insisted I have his last name and she obliged. I could go by Candice, which would seem to make more sense, but my mother yelled it a lot." She shrugged and stowed her thermos in a bag. "And my step-mother always said it in a condescending way. So, yeah, I prefer Candy." Flipping on the light over the sink she grabbed her phone and walked toward the door. "Anyway, there's food in the fridge if you're hungry. Help yourself. I'm going to be late for work."

"Candice Kaine."

As he said it out loud, the reason for the alarms became clear.

Her back straightened, but she didn't face him, just softly said, "Please don't call me that."

"VIP tickets for the chorale."

He was still thinking out loud, not caring about what she wanted to be called. She turned and all the horrible things he

105

wanted to say to her vanished.

"Yes."

"But the website said Krane."

"True. Why?"

"Putting names with faces, that's all. You'd better go."

Jace sat for a long time with his face in his hands. The steam from the tea swirled in hypnotic patterns. He wasn't sure how to reconcile the person on the phone with the woman he'd met. Not that it mattered. The concert was tonight. He would accept Candy's help and surprise his grandma, then take care of business with Raxoco and be out of here by the end of next week. He still needed to talk to Kat about staying with her.

After that conversation, there was no going back to sleep, so Jace showered and sat down at the kitchen counter and worked on the shelter website. Focus eluded him. The phone conversation with 'Candice' kept playing in his head.

By the time Candy returned, his agitation had escalated.

When she came through the door, he said, "I called you." The accusatory tone came out strong.

She looked startled and checked her phone. "I don't have any calls."

"A couple of weeks ago. I called to get a ticket for tonight," he blurted.

Her face paled and she clutched her purse to her chest. "What are you talking about?"

He ran his fingers through his hair. This wasn't what he'd planned, attacking her like this, but who did she think she was?

"You basically said I had no business coming here and that it wouldn't make up for anything."

She stared, blinking rapidly. Then her eyes widened and she shook her head. "No, no. I said those things to … to …"

She paused, "Someone else." The last part was a whisper.

Not trusting anything nice to come out of his mouth, he waited. She put her bag on the table and took a deep breath.

"I thought you were someone else. He sometimes called me Candice, too." Her voice cracked. She closed her eyes, stood straighter, and when she opened them, said, "I'm so sorry."

He immediately felt repentant and said, "I shouldn't have gotten so annoyed by it. I guess I had a reason to feel guilty and that's my own fault, not yours. I'm sorry too."

She retrieved a paper sack from her things, holding it out to him like a peace offering.

"I know it's early, but I brought you a sandwich."

"You know I don't deserve it." His stomach growled in disagreement.

She laughed and waved him off. "Of course you do. You'll need it. Darwin will try to get you to have lunch with him. I'm just giving you options."

They made a plan for the afternoon. Candy had called ahead and would drop Jace off at Darwin's Towing. She would pick up the last of the arrangements for the Chorale. They should be back to her house around the same time. Jace would park in her garage and hang out there until the evening. The VIP seats were in the front and Jace really had no desire to risk being seen, so he opted to come just before start time. After the concert, Candy would get Edie to the back row and feign some errand, which would be fetching Jace for the surprise.

Jace helped Candy load the back of her Jeep with decorations, champagne flutes, and silver trays. He noted the emergency kit and blankets and how impeccably clean she kept her car. Liz had been the opposite and at least once a week Jace cleared out the trash and dirty gym clothes—from both of their cars.

Candy brushed against him as she reached for the button to close the hatch. Desire shot through him. Why hadn't that been there with Liz? Had his relationship with her really been that flat?

Looking back he felt a twinge of guilt. It had been a mutually use-full affiliation. He'd wanted the doors she could open as well as the high-life that went with it—or so he'd thought. She'd just wanted the jet-setter life, no commitment or connection, just a party with her friends. It had worked for a while, until he was too deep to exit with any pride intact. He'd tried for more of a commitment from her, but she had laughed like it was the funniest thing she'd ever heard.

He climbed into the car to go to Darwin's. It was a good thing he would be out of this town by next weekend. Otherwise, the amazing woman next to him might undo all his resolve. One week. He could do that.

Night came and Jace drove to the church. Candy had left a little map just in case. It was a good thing; not much had changed in eight years, but enough that he almost took a wrong turn. He wore some light-colored aviators and approached the door. The usher checked his ticket and told him how to get to the VIP seating. Candy intercepted him before he got very far.

"I found the perfect place. It's close, but in the shadows of the balcony." She took his arm and led him through the back to a side door. Inside, as she had said, sat a couple of folding chairs. He did his best to ignore the emotions her touch invoked, but missed it when she withdrew her hand. "Sorry, they aren't the soft seats, but I didn't want to drag an armchair in here and have people wonder what was going on. I'll meet you outside this door after the performance."

As she walked away, he noticed the Liz-esque heels and frowned. The skirt however, dropped below her knees, something Liz would never have done. He didn't have time for any other assessments. The lights dimmed and the Chorale began.

The music and message touched Jace's heart. He promised himself he wouldn't miss the concert in the future. When it was over, he slipped out and waited against the wall, praying that no one would recognize him. Candy came around the corner, sporting a grin the size of Grandma Edie's heart. She wobbled a bit in those crazy heels as she hurried forward. If not for the obvious delight, the choice of shoes would have irritated him again. As it was, the excitement all over her face dissolved the bitterness rising in his throat.

Behind her, a severe-looking woman pushed a wizened old man in a wheelchair. They gained on Candy and looked like she might overtake her at any moment.

"We are not staying," the woman barked at the man, her lips pressing into a thin line. Jace wondered what was so important that they couldn't pause to soak up the Christmas spirit still hovering in the air.

Concern for Candy quashed those thoughts as the woman moved to pass. Stumbling on a wrinkle in the carpet, Candy came crashing forward eyes wide and her lips forming an "o". Instinctively, he reached out and pulled her up against him so the wheelchair couple didn't run her down as they zipped past. Her warm body sent heat blazing through him. The blush appearing on her cheeks didn't help his situation either.

"Oh," she said disengaging herself. "I'm … I'm so sorry. These stupid heels. I don't know why I thought they would be a good idea." She shook her head, sending waves of silky hair swishing in agreement. Running his fingers through it was definitely out of the question. Yet, the thought lingered. Looking up from her shoes with a sparkle in her eyes she said, "They probably looked lonely in my closet." Her breathless laugh became a conspiratorial whisper. "Your grandma has no idea. Are you ready?"

"Yes."

It was partially a lie. He wasn't ready to let go of her, yet she moved toward the front of the church. He trotted after her, ignoring the reaction he'd had to her, focusing instead on the surprise for his grandma.

The foyer was full of milling people and drafts from the door as the crowd exited. Candy paused just outside the entrance to the chapel, holding out her arm to stop him as she peeked around the doorframe. He couldn't resist copying her. Most people had exited the large room and he spotted his grandma right away. She stood near the last pew, talking to a younger couple. When she shifted to point out something on the far side away from them, Candy grabbed his hand and pulled him into the chapel. He loved the feel of her warm fingers entwined in his and again had to make an effort to think of other things.

They made it behind Grandma Edie as the couple thanked her and headed the direction she'd pointed. She turned toward them. Her expression glowed as she regarded Candy. She barely gave him a second glance. Jace wasn't sure if it was Candy grinning like a Cheshire cat or familial recognition, but his grandma spun back to him. One hand flew to cover her mouth and the other grabbed the back of the pew.

"Surprise," he said in unison with Candy.

"Oh. This… this is …" She eyed Candy with a slight frown. "You knew and didn't tell me?"

Candy laughed. He found himself thinking too much

about her, her obvious joy, her touch, and her concern for others. Maybe he should be more worried about Grandma Edie's scowl.

"It was a surprise," Candy said completely unaffected by the stern look, "and in my defense, I just found out last night."

Jace tilted his head, wondering if maybe he'd made a mistake. Grandma Edie reached out and pulled him into an embrace.

"Oh, my boy," she said. He hugged her back, wondering at her initiation of physical contact. She let go, but kept one arm around his waist and chuckled. "Bet you weren't expecting that."

"No, I wasn't."

"Well, age and Miss Candy here have turned me into a hugger."

He turned to Candy, his eyebrows raised in question, but she merely stared at her nonsensical shoes.

"What about Sunday dinners? Haven't seen any big embraces there."

"Don't want to give your father a heart attack." She smiled up at him. "You know, Candy's been a great help since she moved in next door. Especially these past few weeks." Then under her breath, she muttered, "Too bad she wasn't around when everyone left me."

"Come again?" queried Candy.

Grandma Edie waved Candy's question away. Looking at Jace she said, "I was quite hurt by everyone leaving me."

"Sorry, Grandma." He shifted his stance hating to admit he'd been wrong. "I should have made a better effort to visit."

"Well, there's always the future. And you're here now." Grandma put her hand on her hip. "Which brings us to why are you here? I know it wasn't for me."

Candy nudged her.

"Well? It's the truth."

"Sorry, Grandma, I just never felt like there was anything in this town for me but judgment and after I left, I couldn't face coming back."

"And now?"

"Now, I'm working on a project for Raxoco Resorts."

His grandma put her hand on her hip and stood back from Jace. "That hoity-toity school-wrecking …"

"Edie," Candy interrupted with warning in her voice. Her nostrils flared slightly and her jaw twitched. "I'm going to finish cleaning up. Jace, can you take Edie home?"

The air chilled and it wasn't because the front doors kept opening. Jace didn't need criticism. This job would pay the bills and set up his future. He wasn't risking that. Although he'd thought the same thing when he pursued Liz.

"Sure, but let me help you clean up first."

"It's okay--most of it's done. I just have to do a spot inspection and get the boxes."

"At least let me carry something."

Something about his work upset her, so maybe he could offset it. Shrugging, she walked away.

"I'll wait right here." Grandma Edie plopped down on the pew.

A couple coming up the aisle with their two children stopped. "Very nice job tonight," they said to Grandma Edie.

She patted the children on their heads. A small community had its benefits and this was one of them. He strode to catch up to Candy.

"Did I say something?" he asked a little breathlessly.

They had reached the church's kitchen. She took both his hands and looked straight into his eyes. All coherent

112

workings in his head disappeared. Whatever she asked, he would do it.

"Please, make the most of this time with your grandma. Make it count."

No demands for something selfish? Just concern for his grandma?

She dropped her hold on him, leaving emptiness and held out the box of champagne glasses. The platters were stacked and ready to go as well. Candy picked up a few stray napkins and wiped down the counter before retrieving up the trays. They set their things on a couch in the foyer.

"I'm parked down the block, maybe I should go get my car?" Jace said.

"It's really cold tonight and I'm not too far, I can give you and Edie a ride."

Chapter 11

As they left the warmth of the church, flakes of snow swirled and floated on the arctic air as if they too had been charmed by the music. Candy stepped carefully down the stairs, managing to catch a few glimpses of the fine physique in front of her. Jace paused and offered his other arm. She took it strictly for safety. Trays and purse in one hand, Adonis in the other. He was here to ruin her school plans, she reminded herself. But, if Edie had a wonderful Christmas, it would be worth it.

In the end, did it matter if the community kept the school? She believed it affected more than just her goals. But maybe that was selfish. Maybe she should consider ways she could make this a great Christmas for Edie and her community. Edie's earlier outrage would be overshadowed by her delight that Jace had come for a visit. Even if it was work-related. And the community maybe needed more good, paying jobs.

Snow crunched under their shoes as they crossed to the parking lot. Icy air nipped at her cheeks and she wanted to bury her face in Jace's shoulder for warmth. She clicked the auto-start on her SUV, hoping by the time they got there it would at least be a little warm.

As for her educational path, which was the most important thing in her life, she would figure it out. She would either spend a lot more time driving or move back to the city. Jace lived in the city. Refusing to entertain that thought any more, she moved away from him a little.

She needed to steer clear of him and after tonight, that should be easy. The difficult part would be not reliving the memory of that moment in the hall, the one where she had practically tackled him. The way he'd held her had been so protective. A rush of heat flooded her cheeks again. It had been a sweet moment, but the intensity of her emotions scared her.

An empty double stroller waited to be stowed behind a minivan near her car. The hatch was up and both doors were slid open. Christmas music flowed into the cold night while a mom struggled to get two toddlers in their car seats. Like a game, as soon as one was seated, the other jumped down and out of the car.

"I'm going to see if I can help over there," she said, patting Jace's arm.

He reached for the trays. "Let me take those then."

She handed them over and took a detour to the van.

"Hello, ladies," she said over the music. The three of them stopped. For a split second, no one moved. Maybe an introduction would help. "I'm Candy."

One of the girls giggled. The other, who'd gotten out of her seat as Candy arrived, said, "No you're not." Her round eyes squinted suspiciously, "You're a lady."

The mom smiled and mouthed a 'thank you' as she worked on fastening the other girl's buckles.

Candy grinned at the girl, "If I'm a lady, then you're a princess and all princesses must be safely buckled before the carriage can leave." She patted the car seat. "This is a very nice place to sit because you can see the beautiful kingdom as you ride through town."

"I don't want to go home." She jumped up and down and then out of the van. Candy snagged her and swung her up into the car seat. She thrashed around, but Candy held her firmly hoping the mom wouldn't be angry. "Hey, hey, listen." Candy held still leaning out of the van a little as if listening. The girl kicked but Candy ignored it. "Do you hear it?" she whispered.

115

"Hear what?" the other girl whispered back. The wild one was having none of it, though, and screamed.

Candy, grateful for the many crazy situations she'd faced with her family and in her profession, stayed calm. "Shh. Listen."

The music continued, but somewhere in the night was the faint jingle of bells.

"I hear it." The buckled girl clapped and strained forward. "It's Santa."

"Santa's not coming, 'member?"

The wild girl sat back, pouting. Candy quickly snapped the buckles into place, her heart aching for these little girls.

"Do you hear it?" Candy asked softy. "It's the sound of Christmas, of hope."

The other girl nodded and said, "See, sissy? Santa hasn't forgotten."

Wild girl looked from Candy to her sister and back. Candy nodded and patted her leg. "But you have to be a good girl and you have to believe."

The mom slid the other door shut with a bang. Maybe she'd overstepped, but kids should have hope. And probably adults should too. Meaning her. Maybe she had abandoned hope because it was better than the disappointment she knew was coming. She could deal with that. It was just one year. Next year she would make sure it was different. But this year, she would find a way to do something for this little family.

She slid the door shut and walked around to the back, where the mom was folding the stroller. Her mouth was pressed into a tight line.

"Thank you," she said in a clipped tone, moving so her back was toward Candy.

"What can I do to help?"

"Oh, you've done enough." The hatch slammed down and the woman left Candy standing there. Candy studied the license plate, committing it to memory. She was not giving up. The van sped off, sliding a little as it drove through the parking lot, she only moved to wipe the snowflakes from her cheeks.

Edie's laughter replaced the roar of the van and Candy turned toward her car. Jace and his grandma danced through the snowflakes. She hobbled with her fracture boot, but they seemed uncaring who saw them enjoying this moment. Candy started, they likely had to do it to keep warm since she had gotten distracted by the circus in the van and had failed to unlock her car.

Her cold fingers fumbled with the keys and they dropped in fluff of snow that had gathered since the lot had been plowed earlier that day. Reaching into the snow, she clicked the locks but they were already open. Jace and Edie kept dancing. She was one lucky grandma. The Jeep shut off, requiring her to lock and restart it. This time, Jace helped Edie into the passenger seat and he got in behind her. Candy saw he'd already put the boxes and platters on the seat next to him.

Candy put the key in as Jace leaned forward.

"Wow, that lady had her hands full."

"Yeah."

Her mind spun, trying to figure out how to find the woman, how to help, to give hope to those little girls. All she had was a license plate and she seriously doubted that was enough. She turned onto the street in the direction the van had gone.

"Candy?" asked Edie, "Aren't we going the wrong direction?"

Candy patted Edie's leg. "Ah come on, Edie, I have

barely seen you today. Just hoping to spend a little more time, that's all."

"It's my grandson, isn't it?" Edie smirked.

"Your grandson?" Candy scanned the horizon searching for the minivan. "Who's your grandson?" That ought to throw her off.

Edie thumbed to the rear of the car with a confused expression. "My Jace." She leaned toward Candy and continued, "In your back seat."

Candy glanced at Jace, who looked a little bewildered himself, and laughed. "Ah yes. Your grandson, the absolutely perfect Mr. Jace Marlowe who makes a mean cobbler." She didn't stop the hint of bitterness even though it was undeserved. "I believe I am supposed to be taking you to his car, but please indulge me for a minute."

Silence all around. It was like when Timmy had come at the end of her vision of the first Christmas. She drove the light away. That needed to change.

"I seem to be apologizing a lot lately," she said, noting the corner where the minivan turned. "I'm sorry." She glanced at Edie. "I meant to tease you and it came out all wrong."

Edie nodded and asked, "Where are we going?"

Jace didn't miss a beat, "On an adventure, Grandma."

He leaned up between the seats, sending his masculine scent to the front. The smell faded as quickly as it had come, leaving Candy a little bereft. Jace patted Edie's shoulder.

"But we're together, so it will be a happy adventure," he said.

Chapter 12

All night, Jace tossed and turned on the pillow-top queen mattress in Grandma Edie's spare room. New places did that to people. It had nothing to do with her request that he take her to church, nothing to do with the likelihood of running into people from his past, several of whom he was certain, would be happy to never see him again.

Morning came too soon. Not one to back away from a challenge, he showered, threw on slacks, a dress shirt and tie, and a v-neck sweater. If there was anything Liz had done for him, it was making sure he had a few decent things to wear.

Grandma Edie sat at the kitchen table with some toast and a glass of orange juice. When she saw him, her whole face brightened. It warmed him to the core and completely dissolved the nervousness in his stomach.

"Oh, don't you look handsome?"

"Thanks, maybe a little wrinkled from travel, but I think it'll pass."

"Pass and more. All the ladies are going to be mistletoe green with envy. Mrs. Tarrington might have a festive yard, but it doesn't compare to having you."

"I see your friendly competition with the Tarringtons has weathered another Christmas."

"Nothing anyone pays attention to, dear." She waved her hand at him. "Anyway, here I am chattering away. Can I make you some breakfast? I usually just eat a bit of toast."

He opened the fridge. "I'm sure I can find something."

The shelves were stocked more than he expected. Glass containers held cut oranges, plums, and apples. Others held sliced peppers, celery, baby carrots, and even his grandma's favorite—radishes.

119

"Did you cut all this up?" He pulled the container of orange slices out and set it on the counter.

"Oh no. Candy did that. She worries like a mother hen, that girl, over everyone. She thought I'd be on my feet more than I should, so she took my list to the grocery store, came back, and prepared it all so I wouldn't have to."

His impression of Candy after that horrible phone call seemed way off the mark. He wondered what she would say if he asked her about this conversation. Grandma Edie went back to her newspaper. Jace went back to thinking of Candy as he whisked his eggs. She was the most genuine person he'd met in a long time.

He sautéed some peppers and onion and threw in some ham at the end before pouring the eggs on top. It wasn't a conventional method, but he liked his veggies cooked. He popped two slices of bread into the toaster wondering if Candy liked omelets.

There were things about Candy, like the shoes last night, that reminded him of Liz, but in reality, she was the opposite. She was caring and beautiful and somehow affected him with just a touch. Too bad he wasn't sticking around. Or maybe it was a good thing. He was beginning to think she would be something he couldn't get enough of.

On the way to morning services, Grandma Edie gave little updates on a few people he knew. She pointed out several times that even though some of them had moved away, they still managed to come back often to visit. He nodded politely each time, but refused to comment or justify his own decision to stay away.

The church stood regal in the weak winter sunlight. Memories of many Sundays here flooded in and filled him with both nervousness and anticipation. They walked in together, Grandma Edie holding fast to his arm. It reminded him of the night before, of Candy taking his arm, of holding her in the hall but those weren't thoughts that should precede a sermon.

The smell of damp carpet greeted them inside the large wooden doors just as it had all his growing up years. Jace helped his grandma with her coat. They hung them in the foyer and followed a couple into the chapel. The woman, carrying a small child, turned as she entered a pew.

"Mrs. Marlowe, good morning." She handed the child off to the man, but neither sat. Motioning toward Jace she said, "This must be your grandson."

His grandma stood a little taller nodding as she said, "Yes. This is my grandson, Jace."

He shook hands with them as they introduced themselves. Jace and Edie followed a similar practice a few more times as they crossed the chapel and sat on the far side toward the back. He raised an eyebrow and hesitated. Growing up, they'd all sat together somewhere in the middle. Beside, didn't older folks want to sit near the front?

"Sit, dear."

She patted the seat. He would rather hide on the far side of her, against the wall, with his grandma a welcome buffer between him and the rest of the congregation. Plus, the back wall jutted behind that side of the bench providing even more security. Climbing over her probably wasn't the best idea, so he sat, exposed to the whole chapel.

"Oh, there's Candy." Grandma Edie said in a conspiratorial voice. "I wondered if she would come. She only started coming because I can't drive myself."

Candy looked uncertain, keeping her eyes down. The pale shawl over her shoulders made her look like one of the elderly in the crowd. She happened to glance their way and his grandma took full advantage raising her arm and waving her over. Candy's lips tightened, but she walked toward them, still not making eye contact with anyone. Jace stood to the side of the pew so she could get in. His grandma started scooting toward the wall. That would put Candy between them. A bit of panic twisted inside him. It wouldn't be a bad thing, but people would probably talk.

"Morning, Jace," Candy murmured without looking up.

She squeezed his hand in greeting. You'd think he'd just run to the church with the way his heart beat. It was as unexpected as a bad day on the slopes. In all his interactions with Liz, that had never happened. As Candy passed him entering the bench, he caught the faint scent of flowers. Another deep contrast to Liz.

As was the shawl, Liz not only would never have worn it, she would have ridiculed it. Up close, the thick weave looked sumptuous. It brushed against his hand, confirming the softness he'd suspected. Candy pulled it close around her as she went the last few steps toward his grandma, leaning in and saying something so low he couldn't hear. Whatever she'd said was a miracle because Grandma Edie moved to the middle of the bench, letting Candy sit against the wall.

The reverend stood at the pulpit and started a rousing admonition. Several minutes into the speech, Jace felt the vibration of his phone. Glancing as discretely as he could, he saw an unknown number. Part of him wanted to step out and answer it in the hopes that it might be a new client. The rest of him let it go to voice mail. Moments later, the phone buzzed again. This time it was a text message.

Tried to call. Meet at Hotel Lush to check in 3:30.

He crossed his legs, then uncrossed them, his knee bouncing before he took a deep, calming breath and put his phone away. It would be fine. Andrew would be there and he would politely decline a room if it came to that. Grandma

Edie would be giddy if he continued staying with her. Stretching his arm across the back of the bench, he focused on the sermon.

The reverend intoned about the Wise Men who visited the Savior. They had recognized the sign of Christ's birth, because they had watched for it. They looked to the star, the light, for guidance.

"I encourage you to seek and follow the light of Christ, just as the Wise Men from the East did," he said.

The murmur of several amens followed, including one from his grandma and from Candy.

The reverend then spoke of the magi's journey. They didn't give up during their long travels and they offered Him gifts. Finally, rather than hope for the approval of a king by reporting back to Herod, they heeded the words of God and left the city by another way. He then questioned the churchgoers what they would offer to Christ.

"Today, God does not want frankincense or myrrh." The reverend's voice boomed at this point. "Again, what can you give? Donations to the church fund or local charities. God wants you to take care of each other. Lend a hand or smile at passers-by or even have more patience with holiday crowds."

More amens, but Jace doubted anything in St. A could qualify as a crowd. He shifted in his seat and was about to move his outstretched arm when the back of his fingers grazed Candy's shawl. How could it be so soft? Stroking it completely distracted him from the sermon and when everyone stood, his fingers became entangled. He rose, extracting his hand. Candy raised an eyebrow in his direction and embarrassment flooded his cheeks.

"Sorry," he mouthed to her.

Grandma Edie looked from one to the other, her brows furrowed. Candy's lips twitched and her eyes were bright as

123

she stared ahead. Jace half expected her to burst out laughing at any moment. But she did not. She simply sang the beautiful alto part of O Little Town of Bethlehem. Something about it held a sentiment he hadn't expected. It touched his heart. It had been too long since he'd been away. Away from home, away from God. Now was not the time to be emotional, so he checked his phone. Two more text messages had come in.

Are you there? Please confirm.

Change of plans. 3:00. Confirm.

The day had already been a roller coaster and it appeared that his shuttle wasn't pulling up to the unloading platform yet. He sent a thumbs-up, hoping that would be the end of it.

The service ended and Jace stood. Before he could get out of the pew, several familiar couples his parents' age surrounded them.

Candy squeezed past him, her touch easing the feeling of being under a microscope. "Pardon me," she said. Before she got far, one of the women asked her something he couldn't hear.

The people around him asked Jace about Kat and his parents, how they were liking the city and about Jace and what he'd been doing since high school. It was oddly comfortable. More people stopped, shaking his hand.

"Oh, Edie, this is such a happy day," one of them said. Edie just beamed.

Another said, "Jace, it's good to see you. I heard the powder's excellent, did you come back to ski?"

"Actually I'm visiting my grandma while working on a project for Raxoco." That should go over well. He expected animosity and the crowd to scatter, but it didn't.

"Oh, that's right, they're looking at the old Janssen Manor. That's a great project to be on."

124

They talked a little more about it, but Jace didn't have a lot of details. Opinions were varied in the group, but most thought it would be a good thing.

Their acceptance and friendliness surprised him. He'd expected more antagonism, more aloofness, but no one seemed to remember the trouble he'd caused in high school. The thought came to him that maybe they had let it go.

Back at Grandma Edie's, he'd helped prepare a light lunch and then his grandma had gone to take a nap. With the house quiet, he'd gone over the information for Raxoco one more time, making sure everything was in order. When Jace was finally packed to leave, Grandma Edie hadn't gotten up yet, so he left a note.

Hotel Lush, new since Jace had lived in St. A, sat on a ridge one street up from Main. The name made him think of jungles and green space, but it didn't live up to the expectation. It felt more like a ritzy three-story hunting lodge. The spacious lobby was beautifully decorated in khaki and black. Enormous faux-candle chandeliers hung from the cathedral ceiling and a giant elk rack hung over the revolving entry doors.

Jace sank into an ebony leather couch to wait. A few minutes after three o'clock, Liesl breezed through the doors. Andrew marched right behind her. Jace pasted on a smile and met them at the counter, where Liesl immediately stroked his arm. Her perfume moved with her, overpowering and too sweet.

"How was your stay with Grandma?" she cooed.

Jace moved out of reach and shook hands with Andrew. Liesl didn't even seem to notice. She spoke to the lady behind the counter making sure the three rooms were together. The woman assured her they would be. The pit in Jace's stomach widened, consuming all the air in his lungs.

He redirected his thoughts to Candy and church instead and peace soon diminished the angst.

The desk clerk handed key cards to Liesl and she turned, looking around his feet.

"Where's all your luggage?" Before he could respond, she pointed and said to Andrew, "The bell desk. Get our bags taken up. I'll be in room 325."

Liesl slipped her arm through Jace's and guided him to the elevators.

"Nothing to worry about; you can bring up your luggage later." She pushed the elevator button. "Or we could send Andrew for it." She laughed in her breathless, throaty way while leaning toward him. "I hope it's somewhere far away."

He cringed inside. "Thank you, but I can manage it." The elevator took a long time and Jace hoped Andrew would catch up to them. But then it chimed its arrival. He took advantage of this and extracted his arm to pointlessly hold the door open for Liesl.

Once they reached their rooms on the third floor, Liesl handed him a key-card holder. "You're in 327." She fished out another key, inserted one into her door, and handed the other to him. "If you need *anything*, I'm right here in 325. Come in while we wait for Andrew. If I know him, he won't be long."

Jace handed the key back to Liesl. She raised an eyebrow, but didn't take it.

"If I need anything, I can knock. I don't need a key."

He held the door fully open and waited. Liesl sashayed into the room, flipping on a couple of lamps as she went and then draped herself over a chair near the window.

"Do come in."

Jace swung the security lock to prop the door open. He dreaded being here alone with her. He figured he only had a small idea of what she was capable. The ding of the elevator saved him.

"That must be Andrew, I'll go help him."

Before she could respond, he strode down the hall to find Andrew struggling with a bell cart full of luggage. As soon as he got it over the gap, a flowery suitcase tumbled to the ground. Jace grabbed it and put it back on top of the pile.

"Thanks, man."

Jace steadied a couple of designer cases and assisted in guiding the mountain of bags to Liesl's room. Liesl watched as Andrew distributed her things.

"Thank you." She said from across the room. "Take the rest to your room, and then come back so we can have a quick planning meeting."

Jace held the door for Andrew, praying he would return without delay.

Liesl cut into his musings. "Jace, bring me the black bag, please."

She pointed to a soft, leather messenger bag monogrammed in gold. After Jace handed it to her, she gestured to the other seat and told him to sit. There was no tolerance in her voice. Already feeling the precarious nature of this meeting, he didn't dare challenge her.

The armchair was not as comfortable as it looked, which was a small blessing. It would keep him alert. Liesl rifled through the contents of her bag, pulling out a few thin binders and two pen cases. She handed one of each to Jace and put another set on the table between them. Andrew entered then, carrying water bottles, which he handed to each of them.

"Ah, Andrew. You think of everything." Liesl shot him a promising look that made Andrew smile. "It's a good thing I have you."

Jace cringed inside. This meeting could not end soon enough. Andrew pulled the desk chair over and took his packet from Liesl.

"The first two pages are the itinerary for this week," said Liesl. Looking at Jace she continued, "I'm a stickler for being on time, but that doesn't mean I'm inflexible."

Jace nodded. That was fine with him. A schedule was predictable and with this situation, predictability was exactly what he wanted.

Liesl said, "We will meet in the lobby each day at 8:40 in the morning. Our meeting with the dean is at nine o'clock tomorrow morning. We'll have a tour and then time to discuss our thoughts and ideas before lunch." She pointed her pen at Andrew. "You got the tickets for Monday afternoon?"

"Yes," Andrew said. "Page three. After the agendas."

They flipped in unison past the agendas. In a clear page protector was a voucher for Grosbeak Ridge Ski Resort. Jace nodded, doing his best to look nonchalant.

"Excellent," said Liesl. "Jace, you ski, correct?"

"I'm somewhat familiar."

He did not want to be stuck on the slopes with either of them.

"Grosbeak has the best skiing around and with this weekend's snowfall, it promises to be fantastic." Gazing at him, Liesl leaned in and said, "If you need any pointers, let me know."

Jace shifted away, shaking his head and said, "I'll be all right."

He didn't have to look at Andrew to know the other man's lips were crushed together. Liesl, on the other hand, seemed to enjoy the discomfort of both parties.

"The plan is similar for the rest of the mornings this

week," she said smiling. "Tuesday, the dean has arranged for a tour of the town. I'm hoping we can get some ideas on how to connect to the character and the flavor of this place and incorporate it. It will be a much easier sell if we can do that."

They discussed a few more items in the binder. Liesl checked her watch and rubbed her hands together.

"Any questions, ideas, or comments?" she asked.

Jace and Andrew both responded by shaking their heads.

"Our dinner reservation is in thirty minutes." She motioned to Jace and said, "You can collect your luggage and meet us." Jace rose as she put a hand on Andrew's arm and said, "There's something I need to discuss with you."

He left before Liesl could change her mind. With no time to return to Grandma Edie's, he went to his hotel room. The binder had all the information and contact numbers for the week. Mornings would be the busiest, but the itinerary left most late-afternoons and evenings open. Tuesday after the tour, an early dinner was scheduled with the dean and his wife. Wednesday, regardless of the local week-before-Christmas activities, they had somehow managed to arrange lunch with the mayor and a couple of city council members.

Dinner that night passed without anything unusual happening. Jace drove through the familiar streets afterwards, battling nostalgia. He even stopped at the store and bought ingredients for gingerbread. It had been tradition for him and Kat to challenge Grandma Edie in a gingerbread house competition. It was a two- to three-day activity, though, so the dough had to be made soon. The excitement he felt anticipating the project perplexed him. He reminded himself that a job brought him here, nothing else. When it was done, he would leave.

Chapter 13

Candy refused to sit around and do nothing about losing the satellite campus to a resort. It was Monday and she'd stewed about it after church and all day today during her shift at the center. A resort would bring more people, congesting their streets and shops. Their little town needed education opportunities, not a constant flow of vacationers. Even in the waning light, picketing would be a much better use of her time. And it would mean she wouldn't be home if Andrew ignored her e-mails declining dinner.

Stopping at the drug store after work, she picked up a couple of poster boards and permanent markers. The back of the Jeep acted as a table and it didn't take long to write in bold, bubble letters: 'Yes to Education,' on one side and 'No to Resorts' on the other. She punched holes in the top and strung some yarn so they could drape over her neck.

The gray clouds hung low and air, colder than it should have been, blustered along the streets. It matched her mood as she pulled into a parking space at the school. It was only a short walk to the street in front of the manor. She tucked her scarf into her coat and pulled on her hat and gloves. Needles of cold seemed to find their way in, but Candy was determined to make a stand before she went home.

Patches of snow dotted the sidewalk and her posters barely cleared the snow banks. She paced along the street, waving to cars and doing what she could to draw attention to her cause. Fifteen minutes in, with fingers that felt like ice and cheeks that surely were Santa-red, a car slammed on its brakes and slid to a stop not far from her, hazards flashing. The car behind it started sliding then fishtailed into a spin. Candy was sure it would collide with the stopped car or spin into the oncoming traffic. Someone shouted her name, but she couldn't look away as the car spun to a stop with its tail in a nearby bank. She jogged over to see if they needed help, but before she got three steps, they had gotten traction and returned to the road, honking as they passed the stopped car.

"Candice."

She turned. Her heart stopped beating. Everything in the world stopped moving. Everything except Andrew. His lip curled in disgust as he picked his way over the dirty snowbank and then the recoiled slightly as he surveyed her from head to toe. It didn't prevent him from coming closer however.

"Candice."

Twenty feet away. The air squeezed from her lungs.

"This ..." He waved his arm up and down, gesturing to her getup as he grew closer. "This is beyond embarrassing, beyond acceptable." His nostrils flared. "Go home and get ready. We're already going to be late." He pointed a leather-gloved finger at her. "You." He drew in a breath as he squared up his shoulders. "You always make me late. You know how I hate to be late." A puff of cold breath exited his mouth along with a garbled sound of frustration.

She had replayed many times how things would go if she ever ran into him again. This was nothing like those fantasies. But she was not the same Candy as last year. It was time she stood up to him for real. She closed the distance between them and gently but firmly pushed his accusing finger back to his side.

"Andrew," she said in a calm tone.

What had she ever seen in him? What had her family ever seen in him? Were they so keen on getting rid of her that they would jump on any boyfriend or marriage wagon that came along?

131

The surprise that had briefly surfaced on Andrew's face dissipated into anger.

"Candice. I'm serious." He grabbed her right arm and started toward his car. "We have plans for tonight and you're not going to ruin things. Again."

She pulled back, but his strength continued to propel her forward. Panic shot through her like a crack in the ice.

"Andrew, let go."

Again, she tried to pull away. Andrew's grip on her elbow tightened sending flashes of pain up her arm. There would be marks there tomorrow. He stared ahead as he dragged her along.

"I've had a very trying day." His lips pulled back as he ground out his words, his clenched teeth barely moving. The muscles in his face twitched in tiny spasms. He surprised her by turning and getting right in her face. "And your little stunt is only making it worse. You have a lot to make up for." His eyes narrowed. "A lot."

The streetlights flickered on, subduing the oncoming dusk with a false brightness. Andrew glanced at them and then jerked her back into motion. Her mind raced. If she sat in the snow, he could no longer drag her, but it would ruin her posters and probably her pants. They were almost to the car. Then she remembered some advice Allie had given her. Candy double-timed her steps to catch up to Andrew. With her free hand flattened, she whipped it around straight into his windpipe. A horrible gagging mingled with the sounds of traffic, but the release was immediate. Both his hands went to his neck. He bent toward the snow bank hacking violently.

Straightening, he glared at her in disbelief. "Wh ... what the ...?" More coughing ensued.

She glared back. "I said, 'No,' Andrew. But let me say it again because you didn't seem to get it." She paused as he coughed again then backed away a few steps. She stood a little straighter and stared defiantly into his eyes. "No," she said emphatically. "The answer will always be, 'No'."

Whipping around she started back to where she had been picketing. Her hands shook and puffs of erratic breath danced before her as she paced the sidewalk to clear her head. Andrew hadn't stuck around. That had been a relief. A few people hurried along the sidewalks, but no one stopped to talk to her. The flow of cars began tapering off. Candy rubbed her hands together and contemplated going home. Another fifteen minutes it would be dark and the busy traffic would be over. She couldn't bring herself to call it rush hour. It was nothing like rush hour.

A man approached in the shadows on the sidewalk. All Candy saw was that he carried a steaming cup. Oh, how nice it would be to hold that cup, just for a moment, just to warm her fingers. It was too much. She turned away. Maybe it was time to go home. She closed her eyes. One more pass and she would go to the car. She trudged to where Andrew's car had stopped and, like a little soldier, did an about-face ready to march to the other end of the sidewalk. She stopped short.

Jace stood there in front of her under the street lamp, smiling, a streak of red across his cheeks. Candy had thought he couldn't get any more handsome. Apparently, she was wrong.

Gesturing to his wind-burned features she said, "How was the snow today?"

He grinned. "Perfect. It's been too long and I've been too arrogant. Time for that to change, I guess."

His eyes twinkled and for a moment she let herself get lost in them. A gust blew at her posters and she reminded herself that he was also a dream killer, here to twist her orderly plans into some pretzel of confusion. He baffled her even more by holding out the Styrofoam cup as if it were a peace offering.

"Anyway," he said. "I thought you could use something warm to drink."

The frigid weather made her pride useless. She took the cup, their fingers brushing in the process. Even through her gloves and disdain, little sparks of unexpected energy skipped up her arm. She quickly put her face near the cup, letting the heat seep through her gloves and the steam rise along her cheeks. For a small moment, she savored the sweet scent of tea. He had remembered her preference. Andrew would have brought her a coffee because that's what he liked. Oh, it would be easy to let Jace distract her. Maybe that was his plan. Grateful for the warm drink she regarded him for a moment.

"Thank you," she said, "but aren't I the enemy?"

"Pretty much." He watched the passing cars then said, "It's not such a bad thing for people to go away to college, you know. Cut the apron strings, broaden their horizons."

"It's also not such a bad thing to hide away in a small town, go to school, be part of something," she countered.

"It appears the grass is greener, regardless."

"Perhaps people have different needs or wants. I'm just fighting for those who want the opportunity to stay, for those who want to keep the small-town feel. I'm sorry it also happens to go against your job."

Jace shrugged and pointed to the signs still slung over her shoulders.

"Have you had much success?" No judgment, no condescension. Just a question.

"Not really. A few cars honked, but probably because they think I'm crazy rather than because they agree."

His eyes twinkled with mischief. "So, I have nothing to

worry about, right?"

"Don't count me out yet."

"I wouldn't dream of it." He glanced at his watch. "How late are you going to be out here?"

She sipped the hot tea then said, "Not much longer. Traffic dies down pretty quick and then I'm only freezing my fingers off rather than making a statement."

His mouth twitched in amusement before he said, "True. Where did you park?"

Rather than look around, he waited for her response. She pointed across to her car.

"I'll hang out and walk you over when you're ready."

She waved him off. "I'm fine, it's not that far. Besides you've got too much going on." She gestured at the watch he'd checked.

He laughed. "It isn't that. I'm supposed to pick up some take-out from The Jade Elephant in five minutes. But it can wait until you're done. There's definitely enough to share, so you should come over."

She shook her head. She didn't want to impose now that Edie had her grandson here.

"I'll pop over later to check on her foot, but I won't stay."

"You know she'll eat more if you're there, besides, a warm meal at Grandma Edie's beats hanging out on this street corner."

"Oh, I don't know, it's possible I'd rather freeze my fingers off than watch cheesy Christmas shows."

"If you stayed, maybe we could get her away from those shows, play a game or get that puzzle finished." He laughed, his eyes shining. "Or even start on some dough for gingerbread houses?"

It was awfully dangerous to be around this man. Candy had sworn to be too busy for a relationship. Jace could break her heart in two seconds and she didn't need that. But maybe that was getting ahead of herself. He would likely be gone by the end of the week, when she anticipated Raxoco would wrap things up. Besides it was dinner she didn't have to fix and what better thing did she have going on tonight?

"Maybe."

Jace grinned. "Traffic is almost non-existent," he said as he observed the two passing cars. "C'mon, I'll walk you to your car. Chinese food isn't very good cold."

"True. But it's still a maybe."

She pulled the posters off with her free hand. He reached for them and Candy leaned away. Jace chuckled and even in this awkward position, it was endearing. She wondered what it would sound like if he really laughed.

"I promise to take good care of them," he said.

Realizing the absurdity of her actions, she handed them over. When they reached her car, he laid them carefully in the back as if they weren't a giant objection to his job.

"I'll see you at my grandma's." He would, but only so she could check on Edie.

"All I really needed was this lovely tea," she said as he walked away.

"Don't be late," he called back.

She froze in her spot. Those were words she'd heard all too often from Andrew including tonight. A chill should have gone down her spine, but it hadn't. Maybe it was the mischievous half-smile or the challenge in the slight raise of his eyebrows. She took some deep breaths and got into her car pondering, how the same phrase from two different men could have such opposite effects.

Later, after sharing a quick dinner of Chinese food with Edie and Jace, Candy started cleaning up after both of them. She waved off Edie's offer to help, but Jace came over and started putting leftovers in the fridge. Edie, in what had become routine, hobbled to the couch. Turning on the television, she picked up her Sudoku book and pencil. Maybe a little ennui from too much TV.

"Please stay," Jace whispered. "I don't think I can endure the Christmas romances any longer."

"Then we'll need a plan because she's obsessed with them," Candy whispered back.

"I was going to make the gingerbread dough because it's better if it chills overnight." He paused. "But I don't know if that will work."

Candy remembered that Edie had made them with the kids growing up. She hoped it would bring Edie to the kitchen.

Giving Jace the thumbs up, she said loudly, "Let's make gingerbread." In a more neutral tone she said, "I've never made it before, but I hear you're the expert."

He laughed. And there it was, something Candy knew she would never tire of hearing.

"My grandma is the expert. She taught me how to make it."

He paused holding up crossed fingers. Nothing from the other room. Jace's shoulders dropped a bit.

"Don't worry," Candy whispered. "We'll get her in here."

He nodded and got out the recipe box. They alternated pulling things from the cupboard creating as much racket as possible. Candy retrieved the mixer hoping the sounds would entice Edie.

Soon Edie came into the kitchen. She picked up the molasses and said, "Oh, you're making gingerbread?"

"Come on in, Edie," Candy said steering her toward the mixer. "We need your expertise."

"Oh no, I couldn't. You two are doing a fine job." She

said. "Besides, those stools are a little hard on my back."

Resisting Candy's efforts to get her to sit at the bar, Edie went back to the living room.

"We'll keep trying," Candy whispered wondering why Edie wouldn't want to be with them.

They finished making the dough and stowed it in the refrigerator.

Jace stared into the living room where Edie sat. His shoulders drooped slightly and Candy racked her head to find a way to get Edie back in the kitchen. Jace interrupted her musings.

"Maybe if we get a game going, she'll come in and join us. If that doesn't work, maybe the puzzle or a game of cards?"

Candy paused, thinking. In a low voice, she said, "If that doesn't work, we can be quiet enough she starts to wonder what we're up to." His mouth dropped and quickly shut again. She smirked and said, "Like kids coloring on the walls."

She giggled. If she could ignore the attraction she felt, it could be a lot of fun having Jace around.

With all seriousness, he said, "I'll get a game."

Candy wiped off the plastic covering the puzzle on the table and Jace returned with Rummikub and noisily dumped out the tiles. They exchanged a glance, but there was no reaction from Edie in the other room. Jace won the first game. Candy determined it would be his last victory, no more letting him distract her.

The next game went back and forth until almost all the tiles were chosen. Candy let out a loud squeal and put down her last five pieces.

Edie's face popped around the corner and she said, "What are you two up to now?"

Candy shooed her away, "A horrible, boring game of Rummikub, Edie. You could play, but your show is on and we wouldn't want you to miss it."

"Oh, that. It's one I've seen before, anyway."

Jace paused from turning over the tiles and asked, "Why don't you turn it off and join us, then?"

They played for a while, with Edie winning most of the games. Candy finally pulled off a victory.

"With that, I've got to call it a night," Candy said.

"Already?" Edie asked.

"C'mon, one more?" Jace pled. "And then I've got to go, too."

Candy checked her watch and then started flipping the game pieces. "Okay. But be prepared to go down," she said, looking first at Edie and then at Jace.

Edie had rolled her eyes like a teenaged girl, but Jace had gazed at her with a bit of admiration that made her heart stutter. That diversion caused her to lose horribly. Edie won easily. Maybe she wasn't the only one affected. It was one game night. That was all.

"Edie, do you need anything tonight before I go?" Candy asked.

"No, dear." Edie said, linking arms with her as they walked out of the kitchen. "I think I'll watch a bit of TV."

Edie patted her arm. That little spark of warmth, the one she'd sought since her vision of the first Christmas, filled her. She gave Edie a hug and moved aside for Jace, who waited to say his own goodbyes. Candy headed to the door where she pulled on her coat and looped her scarf around her neck.

"I'll walk you out," Jace said.

They passed his car and Candy said, "Goodnight, Jace."

He didn't stop, nor did he get in his car. Candy paused.

"You don't have to walk me all the way home."

"I know."

Rather than argue, she resumed her pace home until she reached her front porch.

"Thanks, Jace," she said squeezing his hand and running up the steps.

Chapter 14

Hotel Lush's prime spot above Main Street was only a few short blocks from Hearth Oven Cafe. Jace had hit the hotel's workout room early this morning but rather than risk running into Liesl at breakfast, he'd decided to walk to Hearth. He pulled on a dark green beanie before shoving his hands into his pockets and setting a brisk pace. A cold breeze blew at his back and his breath swirled away on it.

Rays of sun stretched their fingers across the valley over the tops of the mountains. Streetlamps still glowed along the avenue, illuminating the giant pine wreaths hanging from each and the traditional red ribbons waved when the wind shifted. Jace caught their balsam scent and breathed deeply. It was a postcard setting and it tugged at his heart. He should have come home for a visit a long time ago. He hadn't expected to feel so sentimental.

Christmas music filled Main Street, ebbing and flowing as he passed the public speakers. Few people were out this early, but later it would be different in many ways. At this time of morning, city sidewalks would be crowded with bustling people, rushing with heads down, to their destination. But here in St. A, the crowds seemed to enjoy the holiday spirit, laughing together, looking at the window displays, and pausing to greet each other.

Jace had never thought he would miss the days with his buddies, running and sliding down Main, weaving in and out of people, throwing snowballs, first aiming to get it through the a wreath, but eventually ending up at the park in an epic battle. One year his best friend Ty had thrown a packed snowball so hard it knocked a speaker off the streetlamp. They'd all pitched in to fix it, but Jace had been grounded for a month after, having to work extra hours at his dad's construction company.

He shook his head against the bitterness of the memory. He'd reached Hearth. The thought occurred to him that although Liesl wasn't likely to be at the cafe, locals would be, and it was very possible that he would run into someone he knew. He hoped the weekend's worth of beard growth would throw anyone off.

The warmth of the cafe swelled around him when he entered. Scents of hot coffee and savory bacon wafted around him and his stomach growled in response. For the first time since he'd left St. A, the contentment he'd sought filled him. He pushed it away. This place could never be home for him.

"Hi, hun, just one today?" the hostess asked.

"Yes, please."

She motioned him to an open table along the bank of windows. It seemed like a prime spot but not many people were there.

As if reading his thoughts, the waitress said, "It gets a little chilly by the windows, so you might want to keep your jacket on." She pointed to a placard on the table. "Menus are there and Manny will be your server. Enjoy."

"Thanks."

He tossed his hat on the bench next to him, grabbed a menu and began looking it over. Out of habit, his eyes went to the prices. He forced himself to peruse the food options and not worry about the cost. After all, Raxoco was picking up the tab. Only once before had he been able to order whatever he wanted off the menu. That had been a rare night when Ty's dad had taken them out after a baseball game in town. He'd admired Ty's dad's generosity ever since. He'd strived to be generous, but with Liz it had always seemed to backfire and he ended up with a gut-load of resentment.

"Jace?"

And it happened. Jace looked up unsure of whom to expect. Surprise filled him as he recognized his best friend.

"Ty!" said Jace. A grin spread across his face, which Ty readily returned. "Have you eaten?"

"Not yet," said Ty. "Was just stopping in for a quick coffee and bagel. I saw you through the window when I walked up. Thought I'd come say 'hi' first, since apparently you're avoiding me."

"What? Never." Jace motioned to the bench across from him. "Have a minute to catch up?"

"You sure?"

"Yeah. I just have to be back to the hotel by 8:30 for a meeting." He paused while Ty sat. "I'm sorry I haven't been good about keeping in touch."

"I wasn't very good either." Ty grabbed a menu as Manny arrived with a pot of coffee and his order pad.

"Coffee?"

"Yes, please." They said in unison.

"Do you need another minute?"

They both nodded then laughed. It was like they were in high school all over again.

Ty spoke after Manny left. "What brings you to St. A?"

"Work. I'm doing the web designs for Raxoco Resorts."

Ty looked up from his menu. "I heard they're trying to buy the old Janssen Manor."

Jace nodded. "Pretty much a done deal from what I understand."

"Don't you care about that?"

"About what?"

"Besides the historical significance, that's where the community college has classes. I know you got out of here to

143

go to school, but a lot of the locals wouldn't go to college if that campus weren't here."

Jace leaned forward. "With what Raxoco is probably paying, they could open two campuses here. It isn't Raxoco who's the bad guy here, it's the college."

Ty shook his head and stared at Jace as if trying to figure him out.

"Can't believe you're defending something like this."

That twisted his gut and suddenly, he wasn't hungry anymore. Anything he said would just be justification.

"What does the community want?" asked Jace.

Ty shrugged. "I just know some of the people, like my neighbor, won't be able to continue school without a satellite here."

"I'm sure there are other places the campus could move to."

"Sure, like your dad's warehouse." Ty shot back. "The 'For Sale' sign is still in the window, just like it has been forever. Maybe you could persuade him to sell."

Jace barked out a bitter laugh. "Like I could convince him to do anything."

Ty shrugged. "It's worth asking." His eyes were intense and he said, "I think there's also a lot of concern over what the resort will do to the manor. It has historical significance and a lot of folks consider it a landmark."

Jace nodded and said, "Absolutely. As far as the Director of Marketing has indicated the goal is to infuse the project with local history and character. I'll certainly do everything I can to encourage them to keep the manor authentic." He tapped his menu. "What do you recommend?"

"Beza's Skillet it my favorite, but Eggs Benny is always a good second choice."

Manny appeared again and they both ordered the skillet.

Over their breakfast, they caught up on their respective families and work projects. Jace skimmed over his relationship with Liz, but for some reason opened up about his dire financial situation.

Ty leaned back in the booth and said, "That's rough, man. But you're resilient. And resourceful. I've always admired that about you. You'll get through it. And if you need help along the way, you just have to ask."

Ty grinned as if knowing Jace's pride would never allow that. Maybe Jace would throw him a curve ball.

"I might need a place to stay. Think Molly'd be up for that?" Ty's grin faltered a bit. Jace chuckled and said, "I'm good for now. Besides, Grandma would have my hide if I didn't stay with her."

"Yeah, especially since I live across the street."

"What? You do? I'll have to stop over."

"Molly and the girls would love that. Plus we could catch up a little more."

They talked and laughed over the last of their breakfast. They parted with a promise to get together again before Jace left. Jace hurried back to the hotel for their morning tour of the town. Following lunch, he planned to go to the historical society and see what information he could find about Janssen Manor. After his experience with Candy and the conversation with Ty this morning, convincing Liesl to keep the authenticity of the Janssen property became top priority.

The morning and early afternoon flew by. Jace took copious notes and some pictures on the tour and at the historical society. He returned to his hotel room with sketches and flow charts and a plethora of ideas, all of which needed to settle.

Jace sat by the dean during dinner. He learned that the dean was looking forward to retirement and traveling with his wife and had no interest in pursuing another location for the satellite campus.

Disappointed by that dead end, he thought about Candy and what he could do. Nothing came to mind. Except maybe persuading her to continue the gingerbread houses. If he hurried they would have plenty of time to cut and bake and maybe decorate them.

Although he'd already eaten, he made a quick beef stroganoff for his grandma. While it simmered on the stove and biscuits baked in the oven, Jace busied himself making a salad. He hoped Candy would stay not only for dinner, but to make gingerbread houses. The dough they'd made waited in the fridge. He also hoped the tea he'd brought her on the street would help his cause. Edie popped her head into the kitchen.

"Smells delicious. Do you need any help, dear?"

Jace opened another cupboard. "Actually, I'm looking for parchment paper."

Opening the pantry, Grandma Edie pulled out the box and handed it to Jace.

"What are you working on?"

"Thought maybe I'd get the gingerbread cut tonight."

"Are you going for the town gingerbread house contest?"

Jace laughed. "Ha. That competition is a little steep so I'll leave it to the professionals. But I thought it would be fun to see what we could come up with here. Maybe do our own contest."

"Just be prepared to lose, dear." Grandma Edie's eye twinkled with excitement. "I might not be as young as I once was, but that means nothing when there's a competition on." She limped over to the table and sat. "I wish Candy would get here, I'm famished."

Jace checked the timer. "We've still got six minutes until

the biscuits are done."

Grandma Edie humphed from her seat. Not that he could blame her, except it wasn't food he longed for. Candy had been completely different than he expected. Nothing like Liz. Not that it mattered, he reminded himself. Besides, he would be leaving by the end of the week. But there was something about her smile and the way she genuinely cared about people that drew him in. At first, he'd thought she simply didn't want the extra drive for school, but he knew now it had more to do with the townspeople who wouldn't or couldn't make that commute.

The front door opened with the customary knock alerting Jace to Candy's presence. The mistletoe that Grandma Edie had hung above the kitchen entrance swayed slightly. Without warning, the thought of kissing Candy under that mistletoe played in Jace's head. It was then she appeared in the doorway, still in her scrubs. If Grandma Edie hadn't been there he would have held up his hand to stop her from coming any farther.

"There you are, dear. I thought you'd decided not to come," his grandma said.

Candy half-smiled and said in a soft voice, "Long day, but wanted to check on you before I head home."

"Come, sit. My foot's been hurting a bit today."

She hadn't complained earlier and Jace wondered what she was up to. Candy immediately went to her. Crouching she removed the boot and sock.

"I don't see any redness," Candy said. "Where is it hurting?"

"It just aches a little."

Candy replaced the sock and boot then slid a chair, over propping Edie's foot up.

"Let's keep it elevated and see if that helps," Candy said.

The timer dinged pulling Jace from his reverie watching Candy. He was grateful his grandma had such a caring neighbor.

Grandma Edie said, "Oh good, the biscuits are done. Candy, will you make me a plate, please? And fix one for yourself too."

Jace glanced at Candy who looked a little perplexed but agreed. Probably wondering why he didn't prepare a plate for his grandma—because that was the first thing that went through *his* head. As they ate, Candy deflected questions from his grandma, asking about her day and teasing her about Christmas movies. His grandma's face lit up.

"Oh, my favorite is on in a few minutes, I'm glad you asked about it. I almost forgot."

Grandma Edie struggled to get up and Jace rose to help, but Candy beat him to it. While she helped his grandma to the living room and got her settled, Jace pulled the dough out of the refrigerator and started cleaning up dinner.

From the living room, Candy said, "Can I get you anything before I go?"

Jace sought for a way he could persuade her to stay and was about to leave the kitchen to talk to her when she appeared in the doorway. Underneath the mistletoe. His eyes went to her mouth. The full lips forming a slight curve tempted him. Would they be as soft as they seemed? He looked up to her widening eyes, finding curiosity and a bit of fatigue, but no apparent objection. He pointed to the mistletoe.

"Grandma has a habit of moving that around. Never know where it will show up."

Part of him felt like when he was young and he and his friends created grand adventures in the woods on the hills. The thrill of fending off trolls, discovering treasure, or the rush of jumping into the icy river.

He watched carefully for Candy's reaction. She still hadn't said anything, just looked up and then back at him. The rest of her hadn't moved. He came from around the counter. Not too fast, giving her a chance to escape if she wanted. He stopped a few inches from her. Her lips had parted.

"Perhaps you will regret it," she whispered.

Oh I doubt that.

The current between them pulled, drawing him closer. Inhaling, she pushed up on her toes and kissed his cheek in the swiftest moment. He didn't even have time to blink or react before she ducked into the kitchen without looking at him. The air stalled in his lungs. Liz hadn't liked his kisses, either. The slow exhale brought no relief. He'd never experienced this kind of attraction to Liz, a desire that threatened his common sense. He wasn't sure he wanted to go where this road led, so it was probably best just to let it go. But he didn't want to let it go. He wanted to have a re-do, wanted to pull her into his arms and pressing his mouth to hers, thoroughly kiss her until there was no breath between them.

Candy didn't speak at first. It was a good thing because he probably couldn't string together coherent words. She began putting dishes in the dishwasher rather than look at him. He watched, wondering if she would stay.

"What have you got planned over here?" She finally asked pointing to the bowl of dough. It was breathless. Maybe she wasn't as unaffected as he'd thought.

In the background, a commercial started but then the TV went quiet. Jace cleared his throat. "I was hoping you'd help me make the gingerbread houses."

She laughed. "That goes way beyond my skill level."

"It's true," Edie called from the other room.

"Grandma." Jace said.

He wanted Candy to stay, wanted to hear more of her laughter. He'd cooked for Liz, but it hadn't been fancy enough, so until their breakup he'd stayed out of the kitchen. "I'm not great either," he said trying to reassure her and certain only his grandma would contradict that statement. "But between the two of us, we should be able to come up with something passable."

"Not great?" She laughed again. "Word on the street is you're amazing and perfect and I can't compete with that."

Edie didn't miss a beat. "True, again."

How many times had Candy endured Edie's stories about him? No wonder she was eager to escape him.

Candy smiled, and he caught a hint of sadness. He wished more than anything to make that go away. She had turned to walk back into the living room. He couldn't leave it like that. Anxious for her to stay, he reached for her hand. They ended up with linked fingers, a gesture that felt intimate yet natural.

Liz would have jerked her hand away, but Candy curled her fingers around his as she faced him. He expected her to let go, but she didn't.

"Grandmas always say things like that," he whispered. "Please stay. You can make your own or we can do one together."

She chuckled under her breath. "Mine will look like those milk carton and graham cracker creations from grade school."

"Care to bet on it?"

"What would we wager?" she asked.

"If yours turns out better than mine, what do you want?"

She pondered for a moment, and a spark lit her eyes.

"If mine turns out better, you stay here with Edie through

150

Christmas?"

He mulled it over, doubting he would be getting a bad deal. More time with Edie also meant more time with Candy. Plus, it would give him a place to stay. "Deal."

"And, if yours is better?"

What he wanted was a real kiss under that mistletoe but he had no desire to come across as shallow.

"If mine is better ..." he paused, tapping the scruff on his chin, racking his brain for something that she would enjoy but also wouldn't want to do. "Got it. You take Molly skiing."

"But I don't ski."

"That's okay, you can always do ski school while she crashes through the black diamonds." Jace could tell by Candy's face that she had no idea what he was talking about. "Bunny hill is easiest, green is moderate, and black diamonds are the most difficult. Ty says she hasn't been the last couple of years, so it would be a great distraction for her."

Candy nodded and let go of his fingers. The void it left was immediate. To seal the deal, she held out her hand. Jace took it and loath to release her again, held on long enough she raised an eyebrow.

"We'll only be able to cut and bake the pieces tonight," Jace said. "We'll have to decorate tomorrow if that's all right."

Candy nodded, seeming relieved. He showed her how to make a pattern ensuring all the sections fit together. Jace couldn't help watching as she meticulously cut the pieces, concentration etched deep on her face. The warmth he felt when she was around disconcerted him.

Without looking up she asked, "How's the project coming? Have you seen the whole building?" She smirked, like she had a secret. Had she done something?

"It's progressing. We toured most of it on Monday." He hated to say anything more, knowing how she felt about it.

Lifting her chin, she leveled a soul-piercing gaze at him. "You can make a difference for this community. You have a way of putting things together that influences the viewer."

His eyes widened at this unexpected statement and he said, "What do you mean?"

She put a hand on her hip and said, "I wanted to know what I was up against, so I looked you up. Your portfolio is impressive, even if your reviews are not."

Oh, sweet terabytes. This was not a conversation he wanted to have. Apparently, she didn't care about that because she ignored his silence and continued talking.

"I left comments of my own, but whatever." She carefully moved her gingerbread to the baking sheet. "My point is, the people here are good people. Like I said before, they care about each other. There is a lot of local talent, a rich history of camaraderie and perseverance." While washing her hands, she nodded to his half-cut pieces and said, "Do you need some help with yours?"

Laughing, he shook his head and glanced at the clock. Regardless of his earlier suspicion, he loathed the thought of her leaving. But they both had work tomorrow and it had gotten late.

"Finish cutting, and I'll transfer them," she offered.

While he worked on his dough, she moved the pieces and cleaned up the stray scraps of parchment paper. With the final section on the tray he put them in the oven to bake.

"Thanks for doing this with me. I know my grandma didn't make one, but I think she'll have just as much fun judging them."

"Which isn't fair, now that I think about it."

She cocked an eyebrow and his insides did little flips. It was late and his resistance to her charm was down. If he didn't take care, he would be kissing her under that mistletoe yet.

"Fair?"

"Edie believes you are perfect, so even if my gingerbread creation is fantastic, yours will be better."

"She thinks the same of you," he grinned at her. "So how is that unfair?"

Candy moved closer and Jace's heartbeat escalated.

"Not true," she said. "She frequently points out my faults."

"Same."

She shot him a look of disbelief and said, "Well the last few weeks, it's nothing but 'Jace is the best at this' or 'Jace is the best at that', so your argument is futile."

Laughing he held up his hands in mock surrender. "We'll have to wait and see then."

***

The hours until Candy showed up to decorate the gingerbread houses dragged, each seeming slower than the last. He was whipping up some royal icing when the knock he'd anticipated all afternoon finally sounded. Candy's normally cheery voice sounded tired as she called out a hello. It was a few minutes before she made her way into the kitchen. Her melancholy expression tugged at Jace's heart.

"Rough day?" he asked.

She flashed a brief smile, but it didn't quite reach her eyes.

"The residents have been a little wild the past couple of days," she said. Setting a reusable grocery bag and her purse

153

on the counter, she waved a hand at the cooked pieces and said, "I'm not sure we should still do this."

"Skiing with Molly will be fun," he teased hoping for a real smile.

As she stifled a yawn, Jace felt a little guilty.

"We can do it another night if that works better for you."

"No, I want an excuse when mine really does look like the milk carton version from grade school. I'll say I was so tired I made the roof into a wall."

The bit of mischief returned to her eyes. Did she have any idea how she affected him? Maybe losing wouldn't be so bad. He didn't have to lose to stay at Grandma Edie's.

"It's on then," he said to her.

They worked together to get the walls up and steady. Being this close heightened his awareness of her. If getting the structure right wasn't such a critical part of the process, he would have completely lost his focus.

When both buildings had their walls up and secured, he said, "That needs about an hour to dry. Want to play a game or watch cheesy movies? Or you could crash for an hour."

She looked at him with such affection that he lost all train of thought.

"That's really sweet. If I crash, though, I might not get back up. How about Rummikub? If I can't beat you at decorating, at least I should be able to pull off a few wins with a game."

Jace chuckled. "Right."

They played for almost an hour while talking about their respective workdays.

"I'm tired of losing, so I think we can do the roofs now," Jace said after three consecutive losses.

They put the sections on and Jace made a bag of icing for Candy.

Handing it to her with a wink, he said, "You're on your own now."

She lifted it in a mock salute. "To your demise."

He vacillated between making icicles and watching her work. She went to the bag on the counter and pulled out a chocolate bell and spray paint. Taking the small gold-lidded canister, she shook it then laid the candy on a paper towel and sprayed it. She hummed Christmas songs as she worked and the happiness on her face went straight to his heart. Once the paint had dried, she glued the bell on the steeple with the royal icing. He needed to up his game and quit paying any attention to the dazzle she had going on.

The TV muted in the other room and Grandma Edie called out, "Are you two ready for me to judge those houses yet?"

"Almost," Jace said.

A few minutes later, he'd put the last of his peppermint discs on the front path to his gingerbread house. Glancing at Candy's church he knew if his grandma picked his, it would be favoritism. The steeple alone outshone his simple house. Candy watched him.

"Your icicles are amazing," she said looking disappointed. "I think your house is way better."

"What are you talking about? Not even close to what you've done. In my opinion, your church is clearly the winner. But I guess what matters is my grandma's opinion. She's the judge."

"Well, I think it's an easy choice." She went to the doorway to the living room and said they were ready.

Jace arranged them side by side and he and Candy stood back. Grandma Edie came in.

"Oh my. Aren't these nice." She examined them, front, back, sides, from several angles and eventually said, "I can't decide. They're both wonderful." Looking from Jace to Candy she shrugged. "It's a tie, there's no other way around it."

"But look at the icicles and the symmetry," Candy pointed out on Jace's house.

"Or the gold bell and perfect shrubs of the church," Jace responded.

"Oh, you two, the fun is in the process. Haven't we all enjoyed it?"

They both nodded.

"So it's a win for everyone. I'm going to bed now. Don't stay up too late."

After she had gone down the hall, Candy turned to him and said, "There wasn't a definite winner, so you don't have to stay."

"You don't have to ski with Molly unless you want to, either."

Candy shrugged. "If she needs a day out, I'd rather stay with the girls, but I will work something out with her."

Of course she would, she worried about other people, so she would keep her end of the bargain. Even if she had clearly won, he suspected she would still make sure Molly got to go skiing. She occupied all of his thoughts for the rest of the night, even after he'd walked her home.

Chapter 15

Icy air surrounded Candy as she and Jace walked from Edie's. Its briskness rejuvenated her. The wind had died down, but the temperatures had remained lower than average. She stuffed her hands in her coat pockets to keep them warm, pulling them out when she and Jace reached her steps.

Making the gingerbread houses had been a fun Christmas activity reminding Candy that family and being together is important. She wondered about her own family. She wished they had these kinds of traditions.

"I had a really fun time tonight. " She raised her arm for a high-five, which he laughingly gave. She continued, "Thanks for helping me."

"I know you had a long day, so I appreciate you staying. It means a lot." He nodded toward the house. "Go get some rest."

As she went up the stairs she determined to be more supportive of Jace's work. Change wasn't easy. She would still be able to go to school even if it meant driving or moving to the city. And in the meantime, maybe she could figure out a way to bring the campus back. Or at least some of the classes.

She found the house dark, quiet, and cold. The dark and quiet she expected. Maybe she'd accidentally flipped the heat off this morning when she turned it down, or maybe she turned it down farther than she thought. Checking the thermostat she didn't see anything unusual, but only cold air blew from the registers. The gas fireplace worked when she switched it on, so it didn't appear to be a problem with the gas.

Too exhausted to worry about it tonight she turned the furnace off. Gathering up her blanket, down comforter, and pillow she went to the couch. Tomorrow she would figure it out.

But she didn't. Two days went by with a crammed schedule. The furnace ended up being last on her list of concerns. Since the fireplace and hot water heater worked, she hadn't made it a priority.

Tonight, like most nights this week, Candy pulled into the garage exhausted. Mr. Lewiston still had family in town, so she had done some light housecleaning and then the swing shift at the care center. It had seemed an eternity of restlessness and demands running higher than usual.

Just before dinner, carolers had offered a nice break, entertaining the residents and getting many of them to join. Somehow, like an avalanche, everything had careened downhill after that. Mr. Tripp had refused to quit singing in his loud, out-of-tune voice. This had caused a certain amount of distress among those in his hall. Candy had quietly stolen Mrs. Green's baby doll, hoping to get Mr. Tripp to see that there was a sleeping baby and that he needed to sing softly. Mr. Tripp had shouted, "A baby!" which set Mrs. Green to searching for the doll. Candy had to slip the doll into the rocking chair and gently show Mrs. Green that the baby was just fine. Mrs. Green wept over the doll and Candy, exhausted, wept with her. Mr. Tripp had been subdued by reports that the nurses had spotted Santa's elves lurking about.

But now she was home with her head against the seat. Solitude and an apparent inability to take care of herself settled around her, a heavy blanket that refused to be discarded. Freezing air seeped into the car with a promise to chill her to the bone if she stayed. Gathering her energy, she pushed the door open. The short distance to the house seemed endless as she trudged along. She probably should go check on Edie but Jace was still in town, so maybe a text would be okay.

No warm air, no pets, no family greeted her as she entered the house, only the emptiness of her life. She had quit checking the mailbox for the Christmas cards that wouldn't come. In all her reaching out she had failed to let anyone in.

The lamp cast a low light into the lifeless space. The only sign that someone lived here was the bedding still on the couch. It did nothing to brighten her spirits. As she switched on the fireplace, a knock sounded on the door.

She panicked for a moment. No one should see her like this. For a second longer, she contemplated not answering but this was Saint Angelo, her family, and someone probably needed something. Opening the door, she found Jace stomping off the cold, a bag hanging from his arm.

"Hey, Candy. I know it's late, but I couldn't wait."

Excitement twinkled in his eyes, spilling over and filling up the whole room. A minute ago, all she'd wanted was to curl up and go to sleep. A second wind must have blown in on a stray snowflake. She couldn't stop the smile as she let him in.

"I can't wait to hear about it." She paused, narrowing her eyes. "Unless of course, it has to do with wrecking my school." The twitch at her mouth might give her away.

The grin he'd sported disappeared and wide eyes stared back at her. She couldn't hold a serious face and laughed.

"I'm kidding, Jace. I want to hear how that's going and I would love to see what you've done so far."

She ignored the raise of his eyebrows and apparent skepticism. "But first, what's in the bag?" She tried to bring back the enthusiasm from a moment ago.

159

"Toys." He held it out to her. "It isn't much, but I figured we could clean them up and use them for those twins you're planning to surprise."

She couldn't believe he remembered. Looking in the sack she saw a couple of dolls, a tea set, puzzles, and some books nestled neatly inside. Some gift bags had been tucked to the side with a pack of tissue paper. He'd thought of everything.

"This is wonderful." Throwing her arms around him, she said, "Thank you." She released him as quickly as she'd grabbed him. "Do you have time right now?" Then it occurred to her that she hadn't texted Edie yet. "What about Edie? I probably should text her. Let her know I'm thinking about her."

Her words tumbled out in an attempt to hide her embarrassment over hugging him.

He chuckled, like he knew how awkward she felt. But it was a warm laugh, not scornful or mocking.

"Grandma is fine, she missed you, but I assured her you were working. She said to tell you she's been keeping off her foot."

"Oh good. She's so happy you're here." Candy hoped he wouldn't wait so long to visit again.

"It's been interesting being back. Not quite what I expected."

"What do you mean?"

They'd entered the kitchen and he looked around as if searching for something. He ignored her question and asked his own.

"Why is it so cold in here? Is there a window open?" He inspected the window even as he said it.

"No. It's just … " She waved him off hoping he would drop it. "Nothing."

What would he think of her irresponsibility in not

160

prioritizing the furnace, especially in the middle of winter? Andrew would have shredded her. She'd looked at it, adjusted the thermostat, but she may as well have been asked to repair a racecar. She'd been too busy to call anyone.

She didn't want to talk about it. She wanted to know what he meant. She reached for some cleaning supplies.

"What has been different than you expected about Saint Angelo?" she asked hoping to distract him as she set the spray bottles on the counter and regarded him.

His fingers drummed a little pattern on the counter.

"I was a little, uh, rebellious as a teenager and I guess I expected people to hold that against me more than they have."

"That's real." She bobbed her head as she considered what he'd said. He frowned, so she continued, "People in small towns are like a giant family. They look out for each other. They care about each other. But you've also got the flip side of that. A bit of backbiting and jealousy over whose jam should have taken the blue ribbon at the town fair. But in the end, you are one of their own and that connection isn't easily severed."

"Thank you for that."

Doing her best to suppress a shiver, she opened the drawer for the washcloths. Jace reached over and took her hand in his. It was strong and warm and sent tingles all the way to her heart.

"Candy."

Don't cry, don't cry. Taking a deep breath, she straightened.

"Your hands are like ice." The word 'ice' came out in a bit of a hiss. "Why is it so cold in here?"

May as well get it over with.

"The heater ..."

Emotions bubbled up, burning in her throat. She shook her head. The shame of not taking care of the situation nearly overwhelmed her. Jace waited, a softness about his expression encouraged her.

She took a breath and blurted, "The furnace isn't working. I've looked at it, adjusted the thermostat, checked the gas supply, those kinds of things."

"So the tank isn't empty," he said more to himself than her.

"It was the first thing I checked. Besides, the fireplace and the water heater are still working fine."

"Have you called a repairman or your aunt?"

Shaking her head again she said, "No. I don't want to bother her. I can't really afford a repairman but I haven't made time to call one either."

"Have you asked one of the neighbors?" His voice was still kind and somehow not condescending. She was certain she would have lost all patience by now. "Or Google?"

"No." It came out as just a whisper as she blinked back the sting of tears. She'd been so busy and so exhausted she hadn't thought to look it up on the Internet.

"Let's go look at it. Maybe it's an easy fix." He laughed a little. "Not that I'm super-savvy with stuff like that, but maybe we can figure it out together."

Candy led the way to a small room in the hall next to the bathroom, flipping on lights as they went. Jace had released her to get a closer look at the heater. Oh that she had a reason to hold his hand again.

"It looks like the pilot light has gone out." He flipped a switch and straightened. "I turned it off. We'll let it sit for a few minutes to let any vapors dissipate and then we'll try lighting it."

He may as well have spoken to her in German for all she

understood.

He moved a bit. "It's a little tight, but come here and I'll show you."

Their shoulders touched, and they kept bumping as he pointed out some valves and buttons. Finally, he put his arm around her only releasing her when he had finished explaining.

"Sorry, I didn't mean to keep bumping into you."

Candy was quick to laugh. "I was thinking the same thing."

"I think it's been enough time. Do you know if there is a grill lighter or a long lighter?"

Candy grimaced and shook her head. "I think over the fridge?" For sure now he would think her brains had frozen solid. She went back to the kitchen to look. Retrieving the step stool, she turned to find Jace with the cupboard open.

"I guess I don't need a step stool if I've got you."

"True." He grinned at her and took her hand, not letting go even when they stopped to turn the heat back on.

Back in the tiny room, he showed her how to turn on the pilot light, hold it, and wait for the flame to take. It stayed lit. She clapped once then dropped her eyes. The scuffs on her boots needed a good polish. She focused on that, waiting for the derisive comments. They never came.

"You okay?"

Pull yourself together girl. He's not anything like Andrew.

Chancing a look at him, her breath stalled. Handsome did not begin to describe him, but that didn't matter. He saw her. For the second time this week, she felt real. Relief flooded through her, comforting and peace-filled. Maybe Christmas was a magical time after all.

She said, "Yes, thank you for showing me how to do that." She would find a way to show her gratitude. "Shall we get going on the dolls and stuff?"

In the kitchen they worked side by side, making the toys look almost new. Sometimes, they scrubbed in an easy silence but mostly they talked about the town and things that had changed.

Candy had washed the last toy in her pile when Jace reached around her. Pressing her between his muscular body and the countertop, he scrubbed a spot on the doll face she had just finished. Her heartbeat raced and she held her breath trying not to think about how good he felt.

"Missed a spot," he said, laughing.

A glance up confirmed the mischief in his eye had returned. He moved away then bumped her with his hip. She nudged him back and wiped the foot of the one he'd worked on.

"Maybe you should worry about your own piece," she said with a smirk.

Grinning, he got the gift bags but Candy tapped the counter biting on her lower lip.

"What?"

"It's nothing, really."

He raised his eyebrows. But she didn't want to make him feel bad.

"It's just the gift bags." It still didn't seem to click. "Can we use them for the mom? I think there's wrapping paper in the bedroom closet. We could use that for the girls. You know, so they could 'unwrap' their gifts."

He shrugged. "Oh course, that sounds better anyway."

"You're sure?"

This time, he laughed. "Yes, I'm sure. Go get the wrapping paper."

She pointed to a drawer. "There are scissors and tape in there."

When Candy returned, he had the gifts for each girl set out in piles.

He said, "Maybe we should wrap them and put them in a bag to keep them separate?"

"Perfect."

When they finished, she resisted the urge to lay her head on his shoulder.

"I really appreciate your help with this," she said

He studied her for a fraction of a second before responding. "You know, you talked about me making a difference, but really, you are the one who does. Thanks for letting me be part of it."

She gave him a quick side hug. "You're welcome." Moving to put a little distance between them, she said, "Now, I want to see what you've got for Raxoco."

"I don't know. I feel like I'm at a little bit of a wall right now. Besides, my laptop is next door."

"I'll wait for you to get it." Still, he hesitated. "Please?"

It surprised her that he agreed. A few minutes later, he returned. He didn't say anything until the computer was set up on the kitchen counter. They sat side by side on her two barstools.

"It's still in the early stages, so keep that in mind."

The landing page was a lovely combination of creams and golds with a navigation bar that was easy to use. It was minimalist and very classy-looking. A photo of Janssen Manor covered in pristine white snow served as the background image. It had been taken at an angle and time of day that made it look like diamond dust had been sprinkled over the expanse of the scene.

"Who did the photo?" Candy asked.

"I did. Why?"

"It's amazing."

"It's not completely untouched."

He winked as if they had some little secret together. It set her heart pounding. Pretending to be unaffected, she focused on the images and links and giving him feedback. He showed her the other pages he'd worked on and they talked at length. As she sat watching him work, the fatigue returned. Her head nodded and she jerked awake. She didn't have time to hope he'd missed it because he stared right at her.

"I'm sorry." His tone was tight. "You're exhausted and I shouldn't keep you up. " He closed the program and shut his laptop.

She touched his shoulder, but he pulled away, standing in the process.

"Jace, stop." The words came out sharper than she intended. She stood toe to toe with him. His eyes twitched a little wider, but he didn't make a run for the door. Good, she had his attention. "I think your work is brilliant. Raxoco is so lucky to have you on this project." She took another breath and continued, "And while I have fought this project—out of my own selfishness, I'll admit—I believe you will be a key factor in Raxoco's success in bringing their clientele to our little town. So please, do not mistake my exhaustion for boredom."

His lips tight, he nodded then said, "I didn't. I just should have been more considerate."

"Seriously?"

Bring it down, Candy.

"Jace?" she said, barely more than a whisper. She hated the pleading in her voice but it was far better than screaming.

He faced her, brows furrowed, questions in his expression.

Maybe the truth would get through to him. "I could have sent you home at any time, but I didn't. I wanted to be with

166

you. I'm sorry." She walked past him to the front door. He followed. "Thank you for your help tonight and for showing me your work. I would love to see more."

"Maybe tomorrow," he said with a half smile.

"I look forward to it. Goodnight Jace."

She pulled open the door to find Andrew stumbling up the steps. Her heart dropped.

"Candice," he slurred. "It's time I got something from our relationship."

Candy tried to shut the door, but Jace surprised her and pulled it fully open. While she was grateful for Jace's presence, he was the last person she wanted as a witness to this confrontation.

"Andrew?" Jace looked from Andrew to Candy.

Had the day been too long or did Jace know Andrew? Her brain struggled to piece it together.

"Jace?"

Apparently, they did know each other. Andrew slipped on the top stair and swore as his knee crashed onto the porch. He struggled getting up while staring at Candy.

"You've been playing me?" Andrew's words ran together in a jumble. The red on his cheeks deepened as he glared.

A little trickle of fear started down her spine, but she ignored it. No longer would this man intimidate her.

She stepped in front of Jace and said, "Go home, Andrew."

Jace moved onto the porch and said to Andrew, "Candy is your girlfriend?"

"Yeah." Andrew sneered for a moment then something seemed to click and he said, "Hold on. Is this your grandma's neighbor? The one you're trying to hook up with this week?" He laughed. "Oh, ho, that's rich."

Candy's stomach twisted as she stared at Jace. His lips

pressed into a line and he shook his head.

Andrew, angry again, stomped his foot and shouted, "Well she's mine, so back off."

Candy checked the surrounding houses, hoping no lights would come on. "Keep it down; it's almost midnight," she shushed him. "And I'm not your girlfriend, Andrew. That ended when you took a detour with my Maid of Honor."

His cold eyes regarded her and he lurched forward. Jace intercepted him, twisting his arm so Andrew's back pulled against Jace's chest.

"Let's go back to the hotel, man." Jace searched the street. "Where's your car?"

"How stupid do you think I am?" He pushed at Jace's grip, but got nowhere. "Let me go. I got a ride and I'm not going back. Get a clue, Mr. Computer Genius, she's playing you too."

"Not true," Candy declared.

Her heart pounded as things started coming together. She moved so she could easily see both of them.

"Wait." They both looked at her as she studied them for a second, then pointing at Andrew she said, "You're in Saint Angelo on business."

"Honestly, Candice. You're so daft. Do you even have a brain in …" Jace squeezed his arm harder, cutting off the rest of Andrew's words.

Candy turned to Jace and said, "You're here working on a project." She gestured to both of them. "It's the same. You work together."

All the air evaporated. Breathing became difficult. She drew in a long slow breath.

Jace said, "Yes." The muscles in his jaw twitched. "And you're the girlfriend Andrew's been going on about."

"Ex-girlfriend. Ex." She hoped her clear emphasis on 'ex'

got through to both of them. Jace hesitated, so she continued, "I hadn't seen him in nine months until earlier this week. He accosted me while I picketed your project. So I throat-chopped him." She glared at Andrew and raised her arm like she would do it again. He flinched.

Jace's mouth twitched. "Let's go," he said to Andrew.

Andrew struggled to escape but Jace held on tight. As they wrestled down the stairs, Jace said, "The boss isn't enough? I'm sure she'll be happy to know that."

The two men scuffling down her sidewalk were like night and day, ocean and mountain. Candy shuddered inside.

"If you say anything, you'll be sorry," Andrew shouted his feet slipping.

Candy watched, a little in awe. She had almost married Andrew who was constantly in motion, slave to the tides of society and his desires. Gratitude that she'd chosen differently filtered through her tired body.

But the gratitude for Jace filled her. He was solid, stoic at times, but down to earth and compassionate. He had never looked through or past her. As musings about him tumbled around in her head, a spark of warmth filled her.

Finally they were too far for Candy to hear anything else, so she went inside and locked the door. Sleep had completely fled. At least the house had warmed up and she could go back to sleeping in her bed. She disregarded thoughts of what could have happened and thanked God for good men like Jace and that he'd come back over tonight.

Chapter 16

Jace had taken Andrew for a suave guy who played fast and loose, but not for a low-life bully. They'd now reached the sidewalk to his grandma's house. What if he hadn't gone back to Candy's? He tightened his grip.

Andrew yelped. "Let go. I can walk on my own."

Jace released him with a bit of a shove. The winter air did nothing to help cool the anger that simmered just below the surface of his control. Jace drew in a long, slow breath before getting in the driver's seat of his car. Andrew glanced over. His lip curled into a sneer.

"If you're wanting some action," Andrew said, his words running together, "that ain't the place." He gestured to Candy's house reminding Jace of earlier.

The memory of the fun he'd had with Candy tonight begged for an argument but Jace refused to respond. Most of him knew that Andrew was wrong, but a very small part of him wondered what Candy's motive had been. She knew he was leaving, so what did she want from him? While he had showed her the work he'd done, she had offered valuable feedback and had seemed interested. Had he read her wrong?

They drove through the deserted streets with cheery Christmas music playing over the radio. Jace fought the urge to turn it off, but had no desire to make useless conversation with the scumbag who sulked in the passenger seat. The holiday decorations along the way contrasted sharply with the somber mood in the car. When they finally reached the hotel, Jace pulled right up to the door.

"Here you go," he said to Andrew.

Andrew fumbled with the door. After a moment, he shoved his shoulder into it. This happened at the same time he managed to yank the handle open and he tumbled out. Mortification filled Jace. He hoped no one saw this awful scene. This would not look good for the company. He'd better get Andrew upstairs before he caused any more of a debacle. Shifting into park, he got out and circled the car, helping Andrew up and into one of the black lobby chairs.

"Don't go anywhere. I'm going to move the car, and then I'll be back," said Jace.

Andrew glared, but Jace ignored it. Hurrying as fast as he could, Jace returned to find Andrew missing. He could now add distress to the gamut of emotions on his plate tonight. Honestly, he hadn't been gone that long. Movement caught his eye and relief surged through him. Andrew stood in the doorway of the office behind the concierge desk.

"All right, Andrew, I'm back," he called

Andrew waved him away. "I'm busy, you go up," he mumbled.

"Should I send Liesl down?" Jace asked. It was stooping low, but after the scene at Candy's he wasn't taking any chances.

Andrew's head whipped around, and his words slurred together, "You're a Class-A tool, Marlowe."

Jace shrugged. Andrew pushed away from the doorframe and staggered around the end of the reception area. They took the elevator up and Jace made sure Andrew went inside his room. He couldn't be responsible for anything beyond that.

Back in his own room, Jace stared at his suitcase. He'd planned to pack in the morning, but too many things were running through his head for sleep to come. The monotony of folding clothes enabled the tide of thoughts to flow. Memories of Candy took center stage, but he shook them off, knowing he would only stay until just after Christmas—that is, if Grandma Edie would let him. He intended to ask her tomorrow.

What if he stayed, found a place in St. A to live? He found himself wanting to stay, wanting to be close to Candy, but also wanting the friendships and genuine connections that St. A had to offer. The freelance work he currently had could be done anywhere. Networking and building a decent portfolio happened more easily in the city. Not that it had really worked for him since his break up.

With the packing mostly done, he lay, staring at the ceiling. Daydreams of Candy ran through his head as he drifted off to sleep. Restlessness plagued him, however. Early in the morning, he woke from a dream of a version of Candy who parroted Liz's old refrain of "You'll never amount to anything".

Resentment ran deep. Throwing back the covers he dressed in shorts and a T-shirt and headed to the hotel's workout room. The familiar exercises didn't distract him from replaying the dream. He knew Candy wouldn't say anything like that but still, it stung.

Thankful the Saturday scheduled only consisted of a breakfast meeting at 10:00 and checkout by noon, he worked out longer than usual. After a quick shower and stowing his luggage in the car, he went to the Business Center at the hotel. It contained two small work stations. No one occupied either spot and Jace hoped it would stay that way. Taking the desk farthest from the door, he opened his laptop and began modifying one of the landing page links.

At 9:55, he walked into the hotel restaurant. Liesl and Andrew hadn't arrived so he asked the hostess to seat him at a table close to the entrance. A few minutes later, they walked in. If Jace hadn't been an observer to Andrew's drunkenness last night, he would have never guessed it this morning based on Andrew's typical impeccable state.

"I like your attention to detail," Liesl said to Jace after glancing at her watch. She shot a disapproving look in Andrew's direction. "Let's order and go over the agenda."

Once the waitress had gone, they all pulled out their binders.

"I've checked with the front desk and arranged a late checkout. We have until one o'clock," said Liesl. "We have an appointment with the Janssen family at two." She studied Jace for a moment. "They're concerned about the hotel keeping the ethos of the manor. While I'm confident your preliminary work will satisfy them, I need you to review it with their concerns in mind. We always have the option of changing something later if we need to."

"We won't need to," Jace said appalled but not surprised. "I think you will find it easy to keep the character of the town and still make it a high-end resort destination."

Liesl's smile didn't reach her eyes and she said, "Just be ready. We are meeting them at the Manor."

The food arrived, ending further discussion for the moment. Jace's appetite had waned. He told himself he would keep this project on track, and he was determined to make a real effort to keep his word. With that commitment made, he relaxed and enjoyed the home-style breakfast.

"Thanks for breakfast and for the week here," Jace said when he finished. "I'm going to the Business Center to make sure the finished pages and the mock-ups are in order for this afternoon."

The meeting went as Jace expected. The ideas and plans had placated the Janssen family. Liesl had reassured them anytime a concern arose. But Jace took note so he knew which details were most worrisome. Andrew had remained sullen and quiet all day and that suited Jace. He had no desire to rehash last night's incident.

When he finally got to Grandma Edie's, her house smelled divine, like she'd been baking all day. His mouth watered. Lunch had disappeared hours ago. He found the living room empty and Candy in the kitchen, cutting vegetables for a salad. His reaction to the dream this morning flared.

"Where's my grandma?" he asked with a bit of an edge to his tone.

Candy turned. The dark circles under her eyes shocked him. It appeared like she hadn't had a great night either.

"She's gone with Molly to get her hair done. They should be back in about a half hour," she said, the words cool. "Aren't you leaving today?"

"That was the plan." He regretted his irritation and reminded himself that Candy was not Liz. "Did you work today?"

"Day shift, then I helped Edie wrap some gifts and bake some cinnamon rolls for the neighbors before her appointment."

Her quiet voice pierced him as she went back to chopping a bell pepper. Watching her, he let the truth of her compassionate nature wash over him. If he were to let her go, he would really be an idiot. He just wasn't sure if she would reciprocate or how they might reconcile living an hour apart and dating. If only she gave him some encouragement in that department. He had dropped hints here and there, like the mistletoe, but she stayed reserved.

The rolls sat on the stovetop, still in the pan and warm from the oven. They needed frosting. He leaned back against the counter.

"Can I help with something? Maybe frost those?" he asked, signaling toward the rolls.

She raised her eyes to his, tilting slightly toward him. His heart skipped.

Candy pointed to a stack of Christmas plates and a bowl of frosting and said, "That would be wonderful. I think she wants four to a plate."

And she went back to chopping. The wall between them back in place.

As he started divvying up the rolls, Candy asked about his day. He told her about the meeting with the Janssen family and how he wanted to make sure things stayed true to the nature of the community and its history.

Candy looked at him with admiration in her eyes and said, "I don't believe it's just fortuitous you're on this project; you're the perfect person for it. The community needs you."

Those words melted all the ire from the night before and his dream this morning. And even some of the frustration from his inability to clearly read her.

"Thank you," he said.

Grandma Edie returned home as the timer for the baked chicken buzzed. Several minutes later, they all clasped hands to say grace. Jace loved the feel of his grandma's and Candy's hands in his—for completely different reasons, Grandma held the past, but he hoped Candy might hold the present and the future. He didn't let go of either after the "amen."

"Grandma, would it be alright if I stayed here for a week or so?"

Candy grinned her Cheshire cat smile. His grandma put her free hand to her chest.

"Are you sure, dear? Because, you know, my heart can't take that kind of teasing."

Candy pressed his hand gently before releasing it, leaving that bit of emptiness where her fingers had been.

175

"I can work from here or the city, but I thought maybe I'd hang around and do some additional PR work as well as the pages for Raxoco."

"Oh, of course, dear. I put some boxes on the bed in the spare room, so we just need to move them, but that shouldn't be a problem. That also means you can help Candy with the Christmas surprise for the twins. You know she's been obsessing over it."

Candy sat straight up. "No, no, Edie," she said shaking her head. "Jace has already done so much to help, plus he's got a lot going on. He doesn't need one more thing to worry about."

"That's not what you said earlier."

Jace laughed. He hadn't felt this light-hearted in a long time.

"It's not a problem; I would love to."

They talked and planned over the rest of dinner. Jace helped Candy clean up. He leaned back against the counter as she pushed the start button on the dishwasher. The collective experiences they'd shared over the week warmed him in a way that he hadn't anticipated.

"You are good for my grandma," he said. *And you are good for me.* "I'm glad she has you."

Candy's eyebrows rose as she regarded him. "Actually, *you* are good for her." Her slight smile widened. "I'm glad she has you. Now, I would love to see what else you've done on the project."

He doubted it would impress her, but at least she would sit close to him. Running his fingers through his hair as he went to get his bag, he wondered if he was getting ahead of himself. She had flirted back a little, but had seemed pretty aloof otherwise. Maybe he should ask about Andrew before completely letting go of control over his heart.

They sat at the kitchen table, where their shoulders brushed as he pointed out different things. Occasionally she offered more than a nod or a compliment.

"It's going to be great once you finish."

She smiled and again, he saw the fatigue. What an idiot he had been. He was so interested in knowing what she thought that he didn't give a care that she was running on empty.

"I'd love to have you test it out as we go, if it isn't too much."

"I would like that, although I don't know much about this kind of stuff. I can barely get through the process at the testing center."

She giggled and if his grandma hadn't walked in, he might have kissed her for it.

"Oh, tell him the story about Hitler."

"Edie!" Candy's eyes widened and her hands covered her mouth. She dropped them and said, "That's supposed to stay between me and you."

"I already told Mrs. Tarrington what a genius you are."

Candy's mouth dropped and Jace grinned and nodded. "Small towns. They have their perks."

Leaning her elbows on the table, she dropped her beautiful face into her palms, the messy bun bobbing as she shook her head.

"The psych class instructor always throws in something nonsensical at the end of every test," Edie said. She took a breath to continue but the commercial on in the living room ended. "Oh, my show is starting. Candy will have to tell you about it."

Candy sighed heavily and told him about several of the random questions, including this last one about Hitler.

"I typed a cheeky answer and threw in some

177

psychological aspects for good measure." Still staring at the table, she said, "I highlighted it to erase it, but instead of deleting, I submitted it." Her voice had dropped. "So, you can see, I'm … I'm probably not a … a good candidate to h-help with any technological p-problems."

The last words were erratic and uttered barely above a whisper. He sensed that somewhere in her life, she'd been berated for things she didn't know.

"I would say you are the ideal person to test. I don't want some overly-clever techie who instinctively knows how to get around a website."

She raised her head, brows furrowed together and said, "You're sure?"

"Positive." Maybe he could bring up Andrew here without being obvious. "It's you or Andrew."

"He'll just tell you what you want to hear."

Jace laughed. This woman was gold.

"What happened between you two?" He blurted it out before he lost courage.

"A lot and nothing." She paused peering at the tabletop again. "He was decent for a while. I ignored the signs that he lived a separate life, even blaming myself when it was obvious." Undoing her bun, she finger-combed and re-did it before continuing. "It wasn't until I witnessed the tryst with my Maid of Honor that I had the courage to walk away." Her chin tilted up. "So, yeah, I'm that woman. I left the church out a back door. I called my Aunt Zathra. She came in like a mother hen and took care of me. So, coward that I am, I've laid low here in Saint Angelo ever since."

"You're not a coward."

She shrugged, "The evidence disagrees. What about you? Girlfriend? Wife? I can't imagine someone hasn't tried to snatch you up."

178

The relationship with Liz seemed as dysfunctional as the one she had gone through with Andrew. He shared the condensed version waiting for her to judge him. She simply put her hand over his.

"I'm sorry it was painful for you."

Maybe it was her own experience that led to her kindness, but he suspected it was simply her nature. He turned his palm up and laced his fingers through hers.

"Sometimes, life is uphill, but you just keep going," she said.

The chair creaked from the living room and Candy released his hand. Edie shuffled into the room as Candy stood.

"Edie, what can I do to get the guest room ready?"

"Just a few boxes need to be moved, dear, and Jace can do that. You should go get some rest. You're starting to look a little haggard."

"Grandma." There was nothing like the honesty of the aged.

"That's where I'm headed," Candy answered Edie. "I have the day shift again tomorrow, so I won't see you at church."

A spear of disappointment shot through Jace. Candy waved goodbye and left. He hadn't wanted her to leave, even though it was terribly selfish. Tomorrow, after her shift, he would find an excuse to go see her.

Chapter 17

Sunday had come and gone in its usual fashion. Now, a day later--Christmas Eve--Candy stood with Jace at the island in Edie's kitchen. She flipped on the light to combat the quickly-falling dusk. The three of them had wrapped the rest of the gifts for the twins and their mom. Edie had gone to find more ribbon, leaving Candy and Jace to finish wrapping. Candy reached for the tape at the same time Jace did, and their fingers brushed, sending tiny sparks of heat up Candy's arm. She did her best to ignore it. Jace would be returning to the city soon. She had no desire to go back and he had no desire to stay in Saint Angelo. What she did desire was him. She just wasn't sure how to go about it.

She had won the tape battle, but felt like she was losing the war. A relationship with him was just a crazy fantasy she had. Pulling off a couple of pieces of tape, she handed it to Jace so he could finish his package. She sighed, not knowing what to do.

"Candy?"

"Hmm?"

Jace regarded her with a serious expression. "That was an awfully heavy sigh."

His five o'clock shadow distracted her, but she laughed off his comment. She hadn't meant to be so obvious and she was not going to confess her feelings.

Gesturing to the gifts she said, "I hope this works."

His smile lit the spark of warmth in her heart and if he'd gone outside, it would have dazzled the entire neighborhood.

"Are you kidding?" He shrugged like he hadn't a care in the world. Rolling up the last of the wrapping paper he swatted her arm with it. "Of course, it's going to work. It's

Christmas Eve." He leaned toward her and whispered, "Everything's magical on Christmas Eve, especially good deeds."

To top off the seductive whisper, he winked. Her heart might just beat out of her chest. It was futile to try to stop the oncoming blush, so she turned away and loaded the tape and scissors back into Edie's plastic organizer. She took a deep breath. She had to stay on track.

"Okay," she said, facing Jace. "We need a plan."

"Yep." He nodded. "We drive up, drop the bags at the door, knock and run." He chuckled. "Like we did when we were kids."

Candy's eyes widened and her mouth opened, but nothing came out. Jace mirrored the action, except he spoke.

"You … you mean you never did that?"

"Never." She shook her head, completely mortified by the thought of ding-dong-ditching. "My dad would have grounded me until I was thirty-one."

"Ouch."

"Yeah. It's all right, though."

"Well, there's no one to ground you now, so tonight we'll let you run wild."

His excitement was contagious, and she grinned as Edie hobbled back in with more ribbon.

"These will be perfect," Edie said. "I'll just get these last gifts prettied up, and then we can drop by Molly's party."

Candy had learned that every year, the block did a Christmas Eve celebration and rotated to a different home for the next time. This year, Ty and Molly were scheduled to host it.

Edie had debated the need for her fracture boot, but Candy insisted.

"I know your foot is feeling better tonight, but it hasn't

completely healed yet, so you need to wear your boot," Candy said.

Jace had sided with Candy and Edie had finally consented. Edie linked her arm with Jace's, leaning on him for support. Candy followed behind as they crunched across the snow-packed street.

At Ty and Molly's, cheer spilled in every direction, from the twinkling lights along the roof to the sparkling lit-up deer on the lawn, snowed in to their bellies. Christmas music sailed along on the tiny snowflakes drifting down the street. As they got closer, Jace carefully twirled Edie around into his arms for a slow waltz up the short driveway, never seeming to mind the hindrance of Edie's boot. Pausing at the end of the driveway, Candy watched in amazement and a bit of jealousy.

Edie laughed and hugged Jace's arm. They entered the garage where the decorations continued the festive theme and he helped her sit in one of the many chairs, decked in red velvet bows and lining the sides of the space. Once Edie was seated, Jace returned to Candy, narrowed his eyes and lifted his chin in a challenge.

"Dance?"

She raised her face to him wondering if he was sincere. She would love nothing more but didn't want him to feel obligated, "You don't have to."

He opened his arms, the mischief back in his eyes. "I know."

She couldn't believe he would. "Really?"

"Yes, really, but it's starting to be awkward with me standing here arms out like this."

She laughed and moved close enough so they could dance. He led her for a moment and a few other couples making their way to the party joined them. Pulling her close, they avoided a collision and kept dancing. The danger had passed, but he didn't move away. Her heart raced and it was difficult to breathe. For two seconds, just two, she would enjoy the faint smell of him and the strength that he exuded. Then she would store it away in her memory for when he was gone.

"Me too. Me too." Molly's six-year-old daughter, Gracie, tugged on Jace's coat.

Candy stepped back, making room, but Jace held onto her hand a second longer. As he released her, she curled her fingertips holding his before her arm finally dropped.

Smirking she said, "All the ladies want a turn with the most handsome guy here."

"My dad's most handsome, but Mom says he'll fall down 'cause he's had too much coffee." She regarded them both and continued, "I can't have coffee. I only get cocoa."

Candy smiled and bent down. "Cocoa is much better, anyway."

"Nope, Daddy says coffee is." She put her little hand on her hip. "Are we going to dance before I freeze to death?"

"There's no competing with that," Candy said, turning Jace over to Gracie.

Smothering a giggle, she made her way deeper into the garage. Molly had gone all-out and the decorations were stunning. Two tables, covered in cream satin and lace cloths, stood at the back. Ivy garlands dotted with frosted berries and peppermint sticks draped from the corners of each one. Hot cocoa, Irish coffee, and wassail took up space on one table while finger foods and a variety of holiday goodies occupied the other.

"Edie, can I bring you a plate of food?"

"That would be lovely, dear."

Candy selected some bacon-wrapped cheesy tater-tots,

salami and crackers, and some fruit. From the desserts, she picked a Santa-shaped sugar cookie and a mini pecan tart. Jace approached as she grabbed a plastic fork and napkin.

"How was your dance?" she asked him.

"All of them were very fine."

She laughed. She hadn't felt so light-hearted in ... maybe ever.

"Well." She waved a hand toward the food. "You'd better get those energy stores up because I'm sure there will be a lot more young ladies wanting a dance."

As he turned away, she thought he said, "There's only one I want to dance with."

She tried hard not to wish he meant her, but she did. Edie took the plate off her hands. "Would you like something to drink, Edie?"

"Wassail would be lovely, dear."

Candy passed Jace on her way to get drinks. "I'm getting Edie a wassail, would you like anything?"

"An Irish, with a bit of English would be perfect," he said grinning at her.

It took a half-second to understand his meaning. Certainly, the heat rushing up her cheeks would melt the snow for blocks. His wink brought her to her senses and she rolled her eyes at him. The hot mugs warmed her cold fingers as she carried them to Edie and Jace. Candy didn't sit; rather, she sipped her drink and made the rounds to greet her neighbors. She loved this tiny community and how everyone watched out for each other. She was talking to Timmy's mom when he came and stood by her.

"Merry Christmas, Timmy."

"It would be a lot merrier if that Marlowe dude weren't around."

His mom's brows furrowed and she shot him a

disapproving look. "Tim."

He shrugged and said in a low voice to his mom. "You said yourself, he's nothing but trouble." He turned to Candy, "And I don't like the way he looks at you."

The unfair comments infuriated Candy. She leaned in and in a voice matching Tim's, said, "That Marlowe dude? He's one of the smartest, most generous people I've ever met. Now, I didn't know him when he lived here, but spreading those kinds of lies is not what I thought this neighborhood was about. Excuse me, please."

Ugh. This was the ugly side of small towns. Maybe the city wouldn't be such a bad option. She could be invisible in the crowds. But she didn't really want to be invisible; she wanted her life to mean something. She crossed over to Edie and Jace, rubbing the ache in her temple.

"You'll get Edie home?" she asked Jace.

"Yes."

His brows furrowed and Edie reached up for her hand. Candy held it for a moment.

"I'm not feeling so well, so I'm going to go home."

"Are you all right?" they asked in unison.

"Yes, just a slight headache."

Turning to Jace, she said, "Come get me later, when you're ready to run wild." Would he even know what she meant?

He nodded and said, "I'll walk you home."

"I'll be okay, I promise. You stay here and visit."

Gracie approached with her sister, Sarah.

Candy grinned and said to Jace, "Besides, it looks like you have some dancing partners."

"You are my first priority," he said quietly.

Her heart melted into a puddle. Waving him off she said, "I'll be fine. These girls need you. It will be much more fun here."

The girls each grabbed a hand, pulling Jace out into the gently-falling snow. Candy laughed as she followed them. He was trouble. Big trouble. Her heart would break because she hadn't guarded it carefully enough. Hugging the girls before they could start their dance, she said goodbye.

Chapter 18

Jace surreptitiously watched until Candy entered her house. He missed her warm smile already. He hadn't meant to get so attached. Leaving St. A would be a lot harder than he had anticipated and his chest ached just thinking about it. The idea of staying enticed him more every day.

Ty's daughters held on to his hands as he twirled them through the light snowfall, laughing at their flake-chasing antics. They were fun, but his mind wandered to what it would be like to play in the snow with Candy.

"Okay, girls." Molly interrupted them. "What do you tell Mr. Jace?"

"But we're not done dancing."

"Say thank you to Mr. Jace, because I just got the news …" Molly's eyes widened and she dropped her voice to a whisper. "Santa's sleigh has left the North Pole."

Jace smiled at Molly's animation over the Christmas Eve news. The girls clapped their hands and jumped up and down.

"Santa, Santa, Santa."

Jace laughed. The excitement was contagious.

Molly, hands on hips, said, "Say your thank-yous and let's go then, Santa can't stop here until you're in bed and asleep."

"Aw, Mom."

"Do you think Mr. Jace is going to leave presents for you?"

Their faces turned serious as they looked up at him, and then back to each other. Gracie's hand clapped over her mouth, as if suddenly realizing that he wasn't magical after all. Sarah copied the action.

"That's right," Molly said. "Now remember your manners and inside with both of you."

"Thank you," they yelled, running through the garage and jumping across the threshold with both feet.

After eating and visiting with the neighbors, Jace and his grandma thanked Molly. By this time, the snow had stopped but some of the clouds lingered. Moonlight burst through a moving cloud. The snow sparkled like diamonds across neighborhood yards and through the boughs of the trees along the street. A frigid breeze swirled the fallen snow into patterns along the street. Grandma Edie shivered on his arm.

"The weatherman said it would turn cold tonight."

Jace wished they could hurry, but his grandma's boot prevented it.

"At least the garage stayed warm for the party." Edie chatted on. "They sure have a nice set-up."

"Yes, they do."

"And excellent food. My fudge bites sure didn't last long."

"Those and the pecan tarts."

"Speaking of tarts, did you see Edna Pinkerton?"

"Grandma!" Jace looked at her in disbelief.

Edie lowered her voice, "Thinks no one knows she's 'had some work done.'" Her arms wiggled as she made air quotes with her fingers. "Looks unnatural, if you ask me."

Maybe she'd had too many mugs of wassail. Jace patted her arm. "Not all ladies can look as good as you do, Grandma." By this time, they'd reached her sidewalk. "Speaking of looking good, the house looks great. Grandpa would be very happy."

"I sure miss him, especially at this time of year."

Jace could only nod in agreement. They had reached Edie's front door. The bags of gifts sat waiting just inside.

Jace checked his watch again. Five minutes until nine o'clock—the time he and Candy had agreed on earlier. He grabbed his keys and auto-started his car so it would at least be a bit warmer when they left.

"Can I get you anything before I leave?" he asked his grandma.

"I'm fine. I'm just going to watch TV and wait for Saint Nick," Grandma said.

He couldn't tell if she was serious. Maybe he should have gotten more gifts, but it was too late now.

"I shouldn't be gone long."

"Take your time, dear. Those girls will be so surprised tomorrow."

Before Jace left, he went to the room he'd been using and retrieved the small package he'd gotten for Candy, 'from Santa'. He hoped he'd be able to sneak it under her tree before they left.

When he opened the door, a gust of freezing air blew into the room. Jace closed the door quickly, not having expected it to be so cold.

"Brrr," said Grandma Edie, pulling the afghan closer around her. "Better grab a hat and gloves, Old Man Winter is vexed tonight."

Jace pulled the beanie down over his ears. His gloves were in the car and would have to wait. Picking up the bags and Candy's package, he took a deep breath before braving the sub-zero night.

The bags fit easily in the back seat of his car. Warm air blew from the vents, but did nothing to ward off the deep freeze happening outside. Tucking Candy's gift inside his jacket, he jogged up to her door. She didn't answer right away, so he did the country thing and knocked again, this time while opening the door.

189

Candy lay curled up under a blanket on the couch. The worry lines were gone and she had a slight smile on those lips that he longed to kiss. She was angelic. He was not at all prepared for the wash of emotion. He wanted her. But he also knew she would never return to the city. And he couldn't stay in St. A much longer. Coming to his senses, he pulled the gift out and hid it in the branches of the tree.

He gave her shoulder a small shake.

"Candy?"

Startled, she bolted upright, smoothing her hair and blinking quickly. She was adorable and suddenly, he felt a bit embarrassed for just walking in.

"Sorry, I knocked, but you didn't answer."

She shook her head as if to clear the cobwebs. "I'm the one who should apologize. I didn't mean to fall asleep. I should have been ready to go." Her words came out in a rush.

He chuckled. "I think we'll be fine. Are you ready, or do you need another minute?" he teased.

Candy looked at him with mischief in her eyes. His heart pounded. Oh, how he adored this woman.

"I guess it's a race to the car, then," she said, jumping off the sofa and moving toward the door.

He snagged her arm and she wobbled a bit, so he pulled her in tight against him.

"You're forgetting something," he said, his voice going husky.

Her eyes widened as she looked up at him. How was it possible for her to fit so perfectly in his arms? He stole a glance at her mouth again. It had parted just enough for a kiss.

"My boots?" she whispered breaking the spell and bringing him back around.

"And possibly your coat? A hat, gloves, maybe a scarf?"

He released her. The absence of her warmth and spirit was immediate.

Faster than any woman he had ever known, she had donned it all and gone out the door. He followed close behind, catching a bit of her perfume. No one had ever smelled that good and no one probably ever would again, so he may as well enjoy it while he could. The wind caught the collar of her coat as she flipped it up.

"Wow, it got really cold, really fast," she said.

Grateful for the small talk, he said, "Doesn't take much when there's no cloud cover."

"True."

Neutral topics dotted their conversation on the short drive to the twins' apartment. A few blocks from their destination Candy grabbed his arm with both hands.

"We need a better plan." It was still cold enough in the car that he could see the short quick bursts of her breath. "What if they catch us? What if this doesn't work? What if they've moved?"

Still gripping his arm, she stared straight ahead as if thinking of all the worst-case possibilities. He couldn't help flexing. She slowly turned, looked at him, then his arm. Her grip tightened and then she withdrew her hand, leaving him again with an acute awareness of the ghost of her touch. He gripped the steering wheel, his knuckles straining against the gloves. *Breathe, Jace.* Why did he have to be so immature? He stole a glance at her, wondering what she was thinking.

Her wide eyes regarded him and her beautiful mouth twitched then grew into a wide smile

She gestured at his arm. "Whatever it is you're doing," she teased, "it's working."

He chuckled. What else could he do? He was an idiot.

191

"Sorry, not my best moment."

"Oh, it was a fine, fine moment," the teasing continued.

He would take it as long as it distracted her. Which didn't last long. They were only about a block away and her breathing had shortened again.

Her eyes now darted back and forth, and her legs bounced in tiny agitations.

Releasing his death grip on the wheel with one hand, he put it on her knee to still the nervousness. His glove muted the touch and he cursed the night for being so cold. Then he cursed himself for wanting her so much.

"It's going to be all right," he said. "Take a deep breath."

Her hand covered his. Now he needed controlled breathing. Her eyes fluttered shut as she breathed deep, curling her fingers under his palm. He moved their hands to the small console between them. They were in this together and he hoped to convey that. He slowed the car and turned into the parking lot.

Christmas lights, frozen into jagged icicles along the apartment's roof, glowed like an alien spaceship. A few of the tenants had lined their windows with lights and a menorah glowed in another. That seemed to be the extent of decorating here.

Jace drove past the building and backed into an empty spot by a set of dumpsters. The BMW would have been out of place, but not his small SUV with its faded paint and cracked windshield. Mountains of plowed snow hugged the edges of the parking lot, blocking most of the lower level from view. They both sat quietly, staring at the upstairs apartments. The light was still on where the twins lived. He tightened his grip on her hand.

"It's a Christmas miracle," he said. A short laugh escaped him as he realized how lame he sounded.

Candy grinned, clearly amused. "Too many Christmas movies?"

She withdrew her hand and leaned forward. With both hands on the dash, she peered intently at the apartments. Still smiling.

Jace wished she hadn't let go. There wasn't any point in dwelling on that, though, especially when they had gifts to deliver. He pulled his focus back to their clandestine purpose.

"This should work out really well," he said quietly. When she turned, one eyebrow raised, he continued, "The night is so cold the mom probably won't venture far to find the culprit of the drop-off." He paused, taking in the whole scene. "Also, they live upstairs, and the door isn't visible from here. Which means we leave the gifts, knock, and run to the car; or we knock and jump down the stairs and hide in the other apartment entry."

The sparkle had returned to Candy's eyes. Maybe the excitement was finally seeping in and it was contagious.

He grinned at her. "Let's do this."

She laughed a tight, nervous laugh. "Are we jumping or running?"

"I vote running."

"I'm good at running. Away." She sighed, her shoulders slumping, but her gaze never left the building.

Jace opened his mouth, hoping his brain could formulate an appropriate response. Before it could, she straightened and turned to him.

"But I'm worse at jumping."

She flashed him a sad smile before opening her door and getting out. A flood of icy air gushed through leaving no time for him to reassure her. He slid out of the driver's seat and retrieved the bags.

193

"Hey, you've got this," he said hoping to ease her fears.

Leaning toward him she whispered, "Best reserve your judgment, I've still got time to ruin it."

"But you won't," he said with confidence.

He was rewarded with a bright smile. "I appreciate that," she said.

The brittle snow crunched as they crossed the parking lot to the stairs. He was impressed by Candy's stealth as they went up and set the gifts by the door.

Using a bit of rudimentary sign language involving pointing and knocking motions, Jace attempted to ask Candy if she wanted to knock. When she nodded, he turned and started down the stairs. At the bottom, he waited while she tapped on the door, then took the stairs two at a time. They ran for the parking lot. Just before they reached the Dumpster, Jace heard the door click open. He grabbed Candy and pulled her into the shadows between the Dumpster and the snow bank.

Her back was against his chest and his arm wrapped around her waist. Neither of them breathed as they watched the landing. The twins' mom appeared, slowly surveying the area, her breath visible by the porch light. A shiver rocked her and she turned to go inside.

Candy's body tensed and she leaned forward. Jace didn't release her. He knew from teenaged experience it was too soon.

"Give her a minute, love." Jace whispered. His lips brushed her jaw. Silently he swore. For so many reasons. The first being that he'd just called her 'love'. The second that he realized he meant it. The third reason was the realization that he was going to have to let her go both physically and mentally. Maybe she hadn't noticed. Her hand gripped his as the upstairs curtain fluttered enough that someone could peek out.

"See?" She nodded against his chest. He continued, "As soon as the curtain falls back, we'll go."

When it did, Jace pushed off the snow bank and they ran to his car, sliding into their seats in unison. Candy held up her hand for a high-five.

"We did it." Her breath became short and choppy, her eyes bright. "We really did it." She shook his arm with both hands and then threw herself back in her seat laughing. "Oh, my goodness, I can't believe we did it." She let out a soft whoop. "That was really awesome." Putting her hand on her chest, she said, "I need to calm down."

Jace chuckled while starting the car and shifting it into gear. This had turned out to be one of the best experiences of his life. Excitement filled the car and his heart.

"Thank you. Thank you," she said, shifting toward him. "I could have never pulled this off by myself."

If she came any closer, his restraint would falter and he would kiss her. But she didn't; instead, she relaxed into the passenger seat and inhaled long slow breaths.

"It was absolutely my pleasure," he said, grinning.

Back at her house, he walked her to the door. The cold air was no match for the warmth of their adventure. At the top of the stairs, Candy hugged him tight for a split second.

"Thank you again. It really was magical."

"Yes, it was."

"Good night, Jace."

"Good night, Candy."

And just like that, she went inside.

Chapter 19

Candy's adrenaline still ran high as she leaned against the door. Was it because he was going back to the city that she wanted him so much? It didn't matter. He was leaving. Yet she would be a better person for knowing him and she would always cherish the memories.

Pushing away from the door, she considered that tomorrow was Christmas. She wanted something yummy to wake up to on Christmas. A cranberry-orange bread braid and hot tea would be the opposite of the usual muffins and coffee that her dad always had available. It would be her new tradition.

She pulled out Aunt Zathra's old cookbook from the cupboard and got to work.

Stirring the ingredients made her arm ache, so she abandoned the wooden spoon and reached in with both hands, squeezing the half-mixed dough through her fingers. She had nearly finished kneading when Molly burst through the front door.

"Hey, Candy," she said, sweeping a critical look around the room. Frustration twisted in Candy's stomach. Who was Molly to judge her situation? Molly raised an eyebrow and continued, "I see you still haven't gotten your Christmas stuff out. Good grief girl, it's Christmas Eve."

"The nativity is out," Candy defended.

"I guess, but where's your other stuff?" She glanced at Candy and then back to the nativity. "Why didn't you say something sooner? My mom has boxes of her old stuff in the basement. I could have brought some over."

"I've been working extra shifts, so that I didn't have time to set anything else out anyway. Did you need help cleaning up? I can come over in a minute," Candy offered.

"No, thanks though, Ty took care of it."

Molly hovered over the nativity and picked up one of the Wise Men, studying it as she came into the kitchen. A trickle of premonition snaked through Candy.

"Um, please be careful, those are Mrs. Marlowe's."

Molly shrugged and set it on the counter. Typical Molly.

"Anyway, I was wondering if you had any dates?" she asked.

Candy hoped she wanted the fruit, not a run down of her social life, or rather, her lack of one. She feigned ignorance.

"Dates?"

Tension rolled through her as she stared into the bowl. The faint scent of orange rose as she kneaded the dough through her fingers. Molly ignored the question and went straight to the pantry. Relief came over Candy. It looked like she'd dodged the dreaded question.

"Dates, Candy. I need dates," Molly said as she moved some boxes around with her free hand. "I wanted to make a fruitcake tonight. I'm too hyped up to sleep and the girls have barely gone to bed. I need something to do while I wait for them to go to sleep. Anyway, I don't have any dates."

"Me neither," Candy said as she continued working the dough.

"Well, I wasn't going to point that out, but since you brought it up …" Candy ignored her, but Molly went on undeterred. "Jace is a really great guy and I think he likes you."

It was like they were in high school again.

"Jace is leaving tomorrow and besides, I'm not ready for a relationship yet." Even as she said it, she knew it was a lie.

Molly made her way across the kitchen picking up the Wise Man again. Studying it she leaned her hip against the

197

counter.

"This smells yummy," Molly said, pointing at the bowl with the figurine. "What are you making?"

Candy relaxed her shoulders, releasing the tension.

"This is for a bread braid. But sorry, Moll, I don't have any dates. I do have some extra cranberries if those will work instead."

Molly wrinkled her nose. "No. I don't like cranberries. Thanks, though." She pushed off the counter, "I'll check next door with Alicia."

"Hey, put the Wise Man back, please." Candy held up her hands, showing the scattered bits of dough sticking to her.

Molly giggled. "I think you need some manly company, so I'll let him hang out with you." With a wink, she turned and headed for the front door.

"N..n..n..no. No. Molly!"

But Molly didn't stop. Didn't slow down, she simply waved as she walked out the door.

The twisting in Candy's stomach returned full force. She didn't need to turn around to know that she wasn't alone in her kitchen. *Calm, Candy, calm.* Deep breath in for the count of four … hold four and don't look … release eight, maybe he'll get the hint. The man spoke before she could start another breathing exercise.

"Be not afraid, child." The voice was low and warm with a slight musical cadence.

There was no ignoring him now. Pivoting to face him, hands still covered in dough, she took in the life-sized version of the nativity's Wise Man. A very large life-size version. His presence seemed to fill every bit of space in her kitchen, leaving no space for the oxygen she so desperately needed. She gulped in some air. *What comes next?* The dark eyes regarding her held no judgment, rather a curiosity, and she thought she saw a flash of amusement. Like Jace. She breathed out slowly. It was going to be okay.

His turban was the same pale fabric as his clothing, although it was decorated with exotic gold filigree and colorful jewels. The luxurious robes covered a long tunic with sleeves that hung to his wrists and a hem that brushed the floor. The edges held a gold design that matched his headwear. The regal magi observed her for a moment then spoke.

"What would be your gift to the Christ child?"

The surprise at his question was quickly followed by mortification. She had no gift. For anyone. She had already dipped into her savings to buy gifts for the twins from the concert. However, this seemed far more important than that.

"I ... I have no gift," she whispered, picking at the drying dough on her fingers.

"You underestimate yourself. You have many, many gifts."

She scanned her sparsely decorated house. There wasn't anything here that she could offer as a gift.

"Not all gifts require money," he said, answering her unspoken question.

She looked back at him and said, "I don't understand."

"There is the gift of forgiveness of oneself and others." He paused as if letting that sink in. "Or perhaps generosity? Compassion? Lifting the burdens of others? A smile? Listening? How many times have you genuinely smiled at someone or paused in your busy schedule to listen?"

The blood drained from Candy's face.

"I've been so busy with work and homework. My grades ..." Tightness squeezed at her chest. "I won't be able to go to school." Tears burned at her eyes, but she blinked them back. She looked at him, silently begging him to understand, regardless of how shallow and selfish she knew her frustration to be.

It had to be her imagination, but she could have sworn he stood slightly taller, indignant at her answer.

"The past is behind you," he said folding his arms across his chest.

She nodded. Bits of dough still covered her hands so she raised her arm swiping the wetness on her cheeks with her sleeve.

"Again, I ask, what would be your gift to the Christ child?"

She took a deep breath. The way she saw it, all those things he had mentioned encompassed one thing, "Kindness." It seemed so right, even as she said it. "I will see people as He sees them. I will forgive, and I will be kind."

A warmth of conviction surrounded her, similar to the love she'd experienced during her vision of the Holy Mother and the Christ child. And oddly, as she pondered about it, during the visionary car ride with Jace.

"That is a perfect gift," the Magi said, his grin revealing the brilliant white of his teeth. He unfolded his arms and gave a sweeping bow, disappearing as he stood. His last words, "You will do well," echoed through her now-empty kitchen.

Only the figurine observed her now. She pondered her experience with the Wise Man as she finished kneading the dough, finally dividing it into two parts. One was for Edie and Jace and one would be for Molly and Ty. She pulled off one small roll for herself. After rolling out and plaiting the dough, she put it in the refrigerator to wait for morning. It was nearly midnight when she finished.

She flicked the deadbolt and glanced outside. Clouds had moved in and dropped a few of inches of new snow. It blanketed the neighborhood, a smattering of rainbow sparkles shining under the glow of Christmas lights. A snowplow cruised past with its orange light flashing. It turned onto the main street and was gone. A car drove by, probably returning from late-night Mass or other celebration.

Her mind drifted to the experience with the Wise Man. The idea of kindness fueled her tired body. Tingling with excitement she donned her coat, pulled on her hat and gloves and went out into the cold.

Retrieving the shovel from the garage she went next door to Timmy's house. Visible puffs of breath surrounded her as she quietly shoveled driveways and sidewalks. Her driveway was all that was left when the clouds thinned and the temperatures dropped even more. Rhythmic sweeps soon had the snow cleared and she finished with a feeling of satisfaction that was entirely foreign to her. The numbness in her chin and nose didn't even bother her, for tonight had warmed her soul.

***

The phone alarm buzzed in the dark of the early morning. Candy struggled, half asleep, to hit the snooze. Ignoring the muscle aches; she snuggled back under the covers. Just as she got settled, her eyes flew open. Last night. Kindness. Bread braids. It all came flooding back to her. But hadn't she done her good deed by shoveling snow last night? She closed her eyes. Five more minutes wasn't long enough to make a difference to the bread. Besides, it was still dark outside and her bed was warm and so she drifted off.

Buzzing startled her out of sleep. *Oh for the love...*

It was a Christmas morning with no gifts and no family to share it with. Why, oh, why should she even get up? She opened her eyes and stared up at the dark ceiling. Contrary to the Wise Man's opinion, she wasn't doing very well. She reached over and shut off the alarm on her phone. The movement sent pain shooting across her shoulder and through her arm. That's what shoveling snow got you. She massaged her arm, contemplating whether to stay in bed, but decided that wouldn't help. She needed to get moving, get those muscles loosened up. Pulling the top blanket around her shoulders, she trudged to the kitchen stopping only to flip the switch for the fireplace. It was the perfect amount of light, except it didn't quite reach the kitchen.

It was too early for bright lights, so she flipped on the light over the stove. The braids had risen a small amount overnight. She set them on the hearth, hoping the heat from the fire would speed up the process. Next, she set the kettle on the stove.

Sipping the tea comforted her and she thought about her family. They would be up already, opening gifts and munching on muffins. Guilt surrounded her. Guilt for not missing them and not wanting to be with them. The Magi's words about forgiveness and her commitment to kindness came center stage. Pulling out her phone, she started a group text message then deleted it. What would she even say to them? Surely, she could come up with something. Leaning her head on her hands, she prayed. This was definitely something she needed help with.

Nothing happened. Realizing she wasn't letting go, she prayed again. A tiny spark of peace and warmth started within her. Once again, she started a group text to her family. This time she wished them a Merry Christmas, expressing love that was genuine and from the heart. It didn't matter how or if they responded. She would be kind. That would be her gift.

With the braids finally ready to bake, Candy brushed a coating of egg over them and put them in the pre-heated oven. She whipped up an orange glaze while it cooked.

Her cell phone chimed a notification for an incoming text. Her dad's wife. Feelings of resentment rose within her. It might take some time to get used to talking to her family again. She looked away to calm her nerves and saw the figure of the Wise Man, still on the counter. She took a deep breath deciding to consider the family fiasco a blessing. She would have married Andrew otherwise.

The message said, *MERRY CHRISTMAS TO YOU TOO, CANDY,* followed by some festive emojis. It was short and Candy was sure it wasn't sent with warm regards.

She let go of the anger, mentally thanking the Wise Man and Jace, and replied, *Thank you for all you do for my family. I hope your day together is wonderful.* She meant every word. All the challenges had forced her to grow and while none of that was comfortable, only Candy could dictate her own actions, could determine to be bitter and miserable or to be grateful and feel love and joy.

The oven timer dinged. The bread was a beautiful golden color and the cranberries gave it a festive flare. She didn't wait long before pulling off pieces of her bun and dipping it in the glaze. The rumbling in her stomach was finally appeased. Once the loaves had cooled, she placed them on a plate and drizzled a generous amount of glaze over them. Time for delivery.

She knocked on Molly's door. Molly's husband answered. He still wore pajamas.

"Merry Christmas, Candy."

"Merry Christmas, Ty."

He opened the door wider. Wrapping paper and gifts were strewn all over the floor and the couches and chairs. The living room was filled with total cheerful chaos.

Candy handed the braid to him. "Wow, that looks delicious," he said, admiring it.

Molly appeared next to him. "Where did you get that?" She looked at Candy through narrowed eyes. "It's not what you were making last night, is it?"

"Yes, why?"

Molly's eyebrows rose. "I honestly didn't think you could bake and I told you last night I think cranberries are disgusting."

Kindness.

Candy smiled and at first it felt stilted, but she let the joy shine brighter.

"That's okay, Moll, you can pick them out."

Candy waved as she jumped down the outside steps a few minutes later. Back at her house, she checked the presentation of the braid for Edie and Jace. Butterflies fluttered. It would be a lot harder to walk away cheerfully if they didn't like it. This wasn't just about kindness. This meant a lot more to her.

Instead of knocking and going in as she usually did, Candy waited on Edie's porch.

Chapter 20

By mid-morning Jace had already packed his suitcase. He put it in the hallway, ready to go back in the trunk of his car with the other one and his bag of miscellaneous stuff from the apartment. He didn't want to leave the stool, but he also didn't want his dad asking questions about a chair in the backseat of his car. And his dad would notice something like that.

He walked out to the kitchen where his grandma sat working on the Dickens puzzle. She might finish it before the New Year. His mind wandered to Candy. She'd put in a few puzzle pieces every time she walked by the thing, almost like she knew instinctively where they went. He pushed the thought away, along with the ache in his heart. He couldn't stay. But maybe the chair would be a good excuse to come back.

"There you are." His grandma interrupted his thoughts.

"Just finished packing up."

"It's been the best Christmas. I'm so glad you were here."

Jace shook his head. "You would have had a fine Christmas even without me."

"Maybe, but having you here was extra nice."

"Do you mind if I leave that stool in your garage?"

Before his grandma could answer, a knock sounded at the door. It surprised Jace, and Edie as well, if the look on her face was any indication.

Jace opened the door to find Candy on the other side. He wondered why she hadn't walked in like usual and gestured for her to come in.

"Merry Christmas."

It was tentative, but who could blame him? He'd wanted

something more last night and she'd walked away. If she didn't want him, he wasn't going to spend two years trying to make it something it wasn't. He'd already made that mistake once.

"Merry Christmas, Jace."

Their fingers touched as she handed over the plate of bread. The usual spark held something deeper this time. It wasn't just physical. Her entire demeanor seemed changed.

"I hope you like it," she continued.

He walked toward the kitchen without looking back and said, "I'm sure we will. It looks amazing." He kept his tone flat, unwilling to give in to her wiles. Edie appeared in the kitchen doorway, blocking him.

"Oh, my dear. That looks delightful." She patted Jace on the arm as she moved out of the way. "I'm full of your pancakes, but that looks too delicious to pass up. Why don't you cut us a slice?"

Candy walked over and gave Edie a big hug.

"Merry Christmas, Edie. I'm sure it doesn't get much better than having Jace here."

"You're right, dear, but it *is* even better than that."

Excitement lit up Grandma Edie's face. When Jace saw how much it meant to her, he wondered why he hadn't made more of an effort in years past. It really hadn't been as bad as he'd anticipated.

"Jace is going to drive me to the city. I'll stay a few days, and then Erin will bring me home."

Candy's grin nearly had him unpacking his bags. He went back to slicing the loaf.

Candy said, "Perfect. A perfect Christmas. And you deserve it."

Jace walked in with a slice of the bread on a plate and handed it to Edie.

"Do you want one?" he asked Candy, keeping his demeanor as chilly as an iceberg in Antarctica.

"No, thank you," she replied looking at the floor. "I had a bit at home."

He felt horrible, but if he warmed up to her at all, he would be agreeing to stay in St. A. Agreeing to whatever schemes she came up with. It went against everything he'd worked against. Besides, his dreams would be stifled if he came back. The little voice in his head argued that he was wrong, but he quickly shut it down and returned to the kitchen.

Jace was grateful that Candy stayed in the other room, talking to his grandma. It gave him time to pull himself together. Soon, however, she invaded his peace.

"I have something to show you. If you have time. I know you're leaving soon, but..." She shrugged looking uncertain.

"Okay. What is it?"

"It's a surprise. You'll need your boots and coat. It's a bit of a hike."

"A hike?" Didn't she know it was the middle of winter?

She nodded, biting on her lower lip. It didn't matter that it was in his peripheral it still burned in his head. How he wanted to bite on that lip himself and taste the warmth of her mouth.

"Sure," he found himself saying.

He reluctantly admitted that he didn't mind spending his last hour in St. A with her. But maybe that wouldn't be long enough. Why did leaving have to be so difficult? It was supposed to be easy.

He said, "We're supposed to head out in an hour." It came out terse.

Candy's shoulders dropped and she shifted her weight as she checked her watch. With a slight grimace, she asked,

"Can we go now, then?"

They took her car and drove to Janssen Manor. She hadn't glanced at him the whole way. Or spoken a word. His heart started to pound. Whatever she had planned, it couldn't be good. Maybe she had lured him here to the woods to … He shook himself. He'd watched way too many crime shows.

But as they pulled around to the back parking lot, doubts started to fly again. Everything was deserted. Candy parked near some stairs, which were covered in several inches of snow. They led toward the trees that bordered the nearly-vacant lot.

"I hope we haven't missed it," she said still not looking at him. "Let's hurry."

He followed her up the steps to a snow-covered path. The snow reached the tops of her boots, but she trudged through it, forging a path. Several times, part of the town showed beyond the spears of leafless trees. It wasn't long before Candy stopped, breathing heavily. He felt a bit of guilt that she had to blaze the trail, even though this was her idea and he had no clue where they were going.

"Let me go in front. But you'll have to let me know where to go."

Holding out her arm to block him, she said, "It's okay, I think it's right here." She hesitated, inspecting the area. "It definitely looks different covered in snow."

She stepped toward the trees. Jace was about to follow when she disappeared below. A scream followed by the sound of branches snapping and then a moan was the only response.

"Candy!" He yelled. "Candy? Are you all right?" All cares about her distant behaviors fled. If she was hurt … but he couldn't think about that. He just knew he had to get to her. He held on to a couple of trees and stepped carefully off

208

the path. "I'm coming down."

"I'm okay Jace. Stay there." Her voice warbled filling him with panic. "It'll just take me a minute to climb back up."

Jace saw her hat first. Bits of leaves and snow stuck here and there all over it. Holding fast to a trunk he reached for her, pulling her up the last few feet. Blood trickled from a cut at her temple. He reached to wipe it away, but she moved past him, forging farther up the path.

"Candy, wait."

She didn't speak, just kept moving. They rounded a bend and she stopped.

"This is it." She said panting. "I should have known."

It sounded more of a chastisement to herself than anything. She stepped off the path and worked her way through an opening. He followed, praying that they wouldn't both slide halfway down the hill before this was over.

A small ledge, complete with a fallen tree for sitting, opened up the view. Roughly a half mile away, the back of Janssen Manor sat regal, surrounded by acres of snow. A bank of tall windows lined the lower level of the building and looked over the valley that stretched out beyond. It was beautiful, certainly, but nothing spectacular.

Candy brushed snow off the log and sat. For the first time, he noticed that her ripped jeans were streaked with dirt and blood stains.

"Candy, your leg!"

She glanced down, concealing some of the tear with her hand. Her focus went right back to the mansion. Her brows knit together and her eyes darted back and forth and up to the sky. How could she ignore it? Maybe the fall had knocked her head harder than she would admit. Jace was unsure of several things, like what to do about Candy's leg, what was supposed to be happening here in the woods, or what he should be looking for out in the fields beyond.

"Maybe we missed it," Candy said.

"Missed what?" he asked, wondering how to decipher the beautiful woman who'd dragged him along a woodland path late this Christmas morning.

And then it happened. The lighting changed. The back of Janssen seemed to glow and the whole thing looked like something out of a fantasy film.

Candy jumped up, pointing, and said, "There." She gave a shaky laugh as she twisted toward him. He could only stare.

"It's ethereal," she said, her voice soft with awe.

"I have never seen anything like it."

"I brought a camera if you'd like to take a picture, but it only lasts a few minutes."

Jace gaped at her as she unzipped a coat pocket and retrieved a camera. Maybe it was Christmas in St. A, or maybe it was almost losing her down the hill, or maybe it was the whole scene before him, but there wasn't a coherent thought in his head.

She shoved the camera into his hands.

"I thought it would help with your project, but maybe I was wrong."

Her words had an edge that brought him around. It took about ten seconds to figure out the camera and then he started snapping as fast as he could from as many angles as he could. Too soon it all faded back to the bucolic panorama. He reached out as if he could stop time, but that was impossible.

Chapter 21

Candy studied Jace, his lithe movements, his focus, his handsome face, committing it all to memory. In a few hours, he would be gone, along with a piece of her heart. Quite possibly the whole of it.

The surreal scene before them ended too soon and Jace reached out to return the camera. She gave him a half-smile as she zipped it back in her pocket with trembling hands.

"Merry Christmas, Jace. I hope it will help you. I'll download them to a zip drive as soon as we get back, so you can take them with you."

The ache became unbearable, but she tucked it away to unwrap when he was gone.

"It was incredible," he said. "Thank you."

They slogged back through their footprints. Candy kept her head down, concentrating on the path and staying upright. Her head and her leg hurt like nobody's business. That's what she got for trying to do something nice. But a few stolen moments with this man who made her feel real made up for the pain. She glanced back and found he had stopped. He stood, staring out at the valley. The contentment on his face warmed her. She shifted her weight to her good leg and waited.

He looked over. His eyes widened and he started jogging through the snow toward her. She chuckled as he hopped along.

"Candy … I'm so sorry," he panted. "Here I am … distracted by the scenery … when you are hurt."

She grinned at him. "That little bunny hop thing?" She asked pointing back along the trail where he'd come. "Made it all worth it."

He blushed and provided one more reason that she would miss him. It took all her efforts not to limp back to the car, but she didn't want Jace to know how badly she'd hurt herself. Certainly not enough for stitches, but she would definitely use a lot of bandages.

Jace apologized several more times on the way home. She assured him it was a minor thing and would take only a few minutes to clean up once she got home. Letting him off in Edie's driveway, she said she would be back in a few minutes with the pictures.

True to her word, she returned shortly with a USB drive of the photos he'd taken. She hugged Edie and wished her a good time with her family, then said her final goodbyes to Jace and to her heart.

The tears started before she entered her house. Sinking down against the front door, emotions overcame her as sobs shook her body. It intensified the throbbing at her temple and the ache down her leg. Part of her wanted to lie on the floor and wallow in the fierce pain. It, at least, partially overshadowed the horrendous chasm in her heart. The other practical part of her forced herself up and to the bathroom to care for the wounds she'd sustained during her earlier fall.

A soak in a warm bath of Epsom salts and some tea tree and lavender essential oil eased the physical aches. But nothing today would lift the weight of losing Jace.

Chapter 22

The drive to his parents' house took less than the typical hour with the absence of daily traffic. On the way, Grandma Edie reminisced about Grandpa Henry. He'd given her wings to fly and she considered that his greatest gift to her. She talked about the bakery he'd started and the many years of work and tenacity it required to be successful. Lastly she mentioned his devotion to his family.

"You remind me a lot of my Henry," she said as they pulled into his parents' driveway.

He patted her hand. "Thanks. He was a good man and I've tried to be like him."

There wasn't as much snow here, but it still covered everything. Jace helped his grandma into the house. After all the hugs and greetings, the sense that someone was missing plagued Jace. He refused to think of Candy and whether she would fit in here. The voice in his head argued in her favor.

Jace's mom ushered them in with hugs and kisses and Christmas greetings. Smells of dinner drifted from the kitchen and Jace salivated in anticipation. His dad offered a handshake then pulled him in for an unexpected hug. Katlyn punched his arm.

"How are things with the boss lady?" she asked, winking.

Everyone turned, focused on him, waiting for the answer. He shrugged, grateful that Liesl hadn't pursued him after the few suggestive incidents.

"Good." He smirked at Kat, who sidled up to him.

"Details, brother, I need details," she said. Pulling him away from the group she asked quietly, "And Erin really likes Ladd, but why'd you dog her?"

The group had followed them and the Christmas music in

213

the background wasn't loud enough to disguise their conversation.

"He's like Grandpa Henry," Grandma interjected grinning. "Only has eyes for one woman."

His mother gasped. "You're dating someone? Where is she? Why didn't you bring her?"

Jace held up his hands to stop the barrage but it did no good. His dad started drilling him, only it wasn't as kind as his mother.

"We're not good enough, is that what you think? Small-town folk with no class?"

"Stop!" Jace's nostrils flared and his fists clenched. "I. Am. Not. Dating anyone." It didn't matter that he wanted to be dating a certain someone.

They all looked at Grandma. She just smiled like she had a secret. It was like a tennis match, as they turned to see Jace's response.

He took a calming breath. "Here's the deal. Boss lady and I work together, that's all."

"But Erin said she …"

"That's not the way I work, and as far as Erin goes, not my type and what she wanted isn't the way I roll either. I'm glad she and Ladd are getting along. And," he glared at Grandma Edie and said, "I am *not* dating anyone."

His grandma chuckled under her breath and hobbled away from them into the kitchen. His parents followed, attempting to get more information from her. Kat looked up at him with raised eyebrows.

"Why does Grandma think you're dating someone?" she whispered.

"The girl next door comes over a lot, so we've hung out a few times." He ached thinking of never seeing her again.

"And?"

214

"And nothing, she lives there, I live here. Life goes on." Well, he didn't actually live anywhere, but at least he had some cash in the bank with which to start over.

"And she'll marry someone there and have their kids and you'll hear about it every month from Grans?"

His stomach dropped, and a cold sweat broke out over his body. Would he feel restless if he went back, long for the city life? He considered that after being away from the city for even just a few weeks, he didn't love it as much as he'd professed. Actually, he preferred the small community. He wiped his palms on his jeans and stared at Kat.

"I think Grans is right, but what're you going to choose?"

"What if she's like Liz and only wants what I can buy her?"

This was probably his biggest fear. Liz hadn't wanted him, just the lifestyle he'd provided because he was enamored with her--the popular girl, an A-lister. She had gotten him off the bottom rung, but it had come with a very high price tag.

Kat considered him, but didn't say anything. In his gut, he knew Candy wasn't Liz. Candy cared about people and hiding behind that community support was a very tender heart. He'd caught a glimpse of it. He thought about them growing old together, sitting on a park bench, sharing a sack lunch.

"Grans is a smart woman." Kat patted his arm and said softly, "It sounds liked you shouldn't let this one go."

He nodded as they wandered into the kitchen where the others had already started loading plates with food. Somehow, he would figure it out.

A festive cloth protected the buffet table his dad had made for his mom when they were newly married. Savory ham, sliced turkey, sauces, gravies, vegetables, and a fruit salad occupied various spots.

"This looks amazing, Mom," Jace said.

With her plate in one hand, she gave him a little side hug with the other. "It's good to be together." She nudged his dad.

"Sorry about my outburst."

Jace's mouth dropped open and his mother shot him a warning look. He closed it and said, "Thanks, Dad." It was all he could say. He didn't remember his dad every apologizing for anything. Ever.

After dinner, the group exchanged gifts while his mom took a thousand pictures. Online shopping and two-day delivery had saved his bacon this Christmas. The appreciation on his parents' face when they opened their gifts warmed him and seemed to dissolve any ire from when he'd arrived.

His dad turned on a football game. The half-time show had just ended. Grandma and his mom went to the kitchen. Jace followed to see if he could help, but they shooed him back to the living room. Kat had curled up on one end of the couch and had started reading one of the books she'd gotten. He took the other end near his dad.

They watched and talked football. They cheered as their preferred team intercepted the ball with thirty seconds left in the game. They needed a touchdown to win the game. With five seconds left, the quarterback threw a pass. The receiver bobbled it over his head. It bounced off the helmet of the opposing team. The tight end snatched it and dove across the goal line. Jace and his dad jumped up, whooping and high-fiving each other.

"Time for dessert," his mom called from the kitchen.

Several pies lined the counter. Each had a small spatula stuck under a slice. A bowl of whipped cream and a container of vanilla bean ice cream waited at the end.

Jace lingered behind until the rest of the family had cut and scooped their desserts.

"Grandma, tell me which kind would you like and I'll get it for you."

"Thank you, dear. Let's do a small slice of cherry and peach."

This got an eyebrow raise from his mom, but no comment. After getting Grandma Edie's pies dished up, he cut a large slice of his favorite—peach—then added a double scoop of ice cream. He wanted to go to the living room with its quiet solitude, but he joined his family at the table. They hadn't even had a chance to get the conversation going when the doorbell rang. His dad got up to answer it and returned with a couple.

"I'd like you to meet our neighbors, Bob and Rosa Wixom."

His dad introduced each of the family members, and then pointed to the pie. "What can I get for you?"

Jace was surprised when Rosa waved his dad off and said, "You go sit. We can manage over here."

When they joined them, Jace's dad said, "How's the merger, Bob?"

Their conversation went on about business and the advantage this move would be for Bob's company. Unfortunately, it wouldn't be a benefit for all the employees, as one of the locations had to close. Jace felt a kinship to those people and hoped they would be able to find work quickly.

Mrs. Wixom talked a moment to Erin asking about her job and social life. As long as Erin kept her engaged, it would be perfect. Jace did not want to answer those same questions, especially in front of his parents. He had almost finished eating when Mrs. Wixom leaned his direction and did the very thing he'd dreaded.

"How about you, Jace? What do you do for work?"

He swallowed, taking his time to respond. "I work in IT."

"Oh? Whom do you work for?"

"I'm currently on a project for Raxoco Resorts and have a couple of other smaller clients."

She nodded, took another bite of pie, and assessed him. He cursed the other conversations for going quiet at just this moment. Luck must really hate him.

"He's really good at what he does," Erin piped in. "Graduated the top of his class."

Mrs. Wixom said, "Would you ever consider teaching?"

He paused with his spoon halfway to his mouth then set it down. "I hadn't thought about it, but I wouldn't rule it out."

She looked at Jace's dad and said, "You didn't tell me this." Then, back to Jace, "Do you have a resume? A portfolio?"

"Yes." He hesitated. How to handle this without destroying his chance and without adding weapons to his dad's arsenal? Best stick with the truth. "I can send you my resume as well as my portfolio. But I have to warn you, you will likely find a lot of misinformation if you go digging." When she raised an eyebrow, he shrugged and simply said, "Bad breakup."

She didn't seem put off by it. "Aren't you interested in whom I work for?"

Jace felt like an idiot. "Of course, tell me about your company."

"I'm the president of Mack Community College." She didn't say any more, it was like she was waiting for it to sink into his head. Then she gestured toward his dad and said, "I talked with your dad last week. Raxoco is indeed making a

218

push to buy the current location of our satellite campus in Saint Angelo. We were unsure about keeping a campus in Saint Angelo. After our conversation," she said with a nod to Dad, "I spoke to the Board and we all agree that if we could find a solution, it would benefit everyone to keep a campus there."

The air seemed to have left the room, but he managed to say to his dad, "Why didn't you say anything?"

"I spoke with Rosa after we talked and you didn't ask."

Typical Dad response.

Mrs. Wixom smiled warmly. "Your dad suggested a vacant warehouse. I believe it used to be an old bakery."

"Henry's old building? Oh that will be perfect," his grandma chimed in.

Mrs. Wixom continued, "We think it will facilitate a much better use of our funds." All focus was on her and she seemed to be enjoying the limelight, or perhaps it was the Christmas spirit. She continued, all cheerful, "The drawbacks are few. It will take some time to renovate the building—we also need an architect, but that's another matter. I will need more faculty and staff." She pointed at Jace. "That's where I'm hoping you come in. We currently don't have IT classes at that campus and the college's Information Officer is retiring at the end of Spring semester. It puts me in a bit of a bind, actually."

Her eyes narrowed as she stared at her half-eaten dessert. Then she turned that look on Jace. "Liesl Thomas can be ... a bit challenging, but she knows her stuff. I didn't realize that the computer guy she raved about was my neighbor's son. I'm willing to offer you a similar job. Only it would be for the warehouse project. I am also willing to offer a teaching position. I've got an entry-level class at the main campus that I need an instructor for. If it works out, it would extend to the Saint Angelo location once it's open; that position would also be over Information Technology for the entire satellite campus."

Jace didn't need time to think about it. The whole drive away from St. A had filled him with regret. It wasn't until he had to leave that he appreciated what was there. He suspected it had more to do with a beautiful nursing student than he wanted to admit, but the connections there—with Ty and Molly, with the people in town—had been unexpected and real. Candy was right; it was like a big family. It was where he wanted to be. Hope had come through for him. It truly was a Christmas miracle.

"I accept." He shook Mrs. Wixom's hand and said, "I also know an excellent architect."

He couldn't wait to tell Candy. And maybe pursue that relationship as well. He hesitated only because he didn't know if his interest in something long-term was reciprocated.

Chapter 23

After cleaning up her wounds and admitting that Edie and Jace had gone, loneliness pressed around Candy. Combating it the only way she knew, she baked up some Christmas sugar cookies. When they had cooled, she frosted and plated them on festive paper plates. Their merriness was the opposite of how she felt. She decided to stop at Miss Stacey's first.

Her daughter Carolyn answered the door. It was a picture similar to Ty and Molly's earlier. A trash bag stuffed with wrapping paper leaned against the couch and several kids ran out of the room as the last one counted loudly. A football game was on and while several adults sat watching, a couple of people visited with each other.

"Just wanted to deliver these and wish Miss Stacey a Merry Christmas," Candy said handing the plate to Carolyn.

Miss Stacey appeared from the kitchen. "Miss Candy, that's so sweet. How's your Christmas?"

Carolyn took the goodies and left them to scold some younger children. "Wonderful, of course. I was just dropping by to a few of my favorite people. Mr. Lewiston is next on my list," she said, wondering if Miss Stacey would take the bait.

Her eyes widened and she glanced behind her before she whispered, "Do you think they'd notice if I disappeared for a bit?"

Candy chuckled and shook her head. "Probably not," she said softly. "The game is on and the kids are happy, but maybe we should tell Carolyn."

They escaped with only Carolyn the wiser.

A few cars had parked in front of Mr. Lewiston's home.

Candy parked next to one in the driveway. Miss Stacey fidgeted as she peered at the house.

Candy shut off the car and said, "Don't worry, we've got this. It will be fine."

They walked arm-in-arm to the door. Candy balanced the plate of cookies in her other hand. Mr. Lewiston answered. The surprise on his face was worth all the effort of her scheming.

"Come in, come in," he said opening the door wide.

They went inside and Candy gave him the plate of cookies. He handed them off to his only daughter, whom Candy had already met.

"Lyla, you've already met Candy, but this is her friend, Miss Stacey."

"Come on in," she said with an enthusiastic smile. Happy squeals came from the other room and Lyla shook her head. "Sorry, it's a bit crazy around here."

Miss Stacey laughed, "Isn't it everywhere?"

Candy's heart hitched. *Except my house. Someday,* she told herself.

Mr. Lewiston waved some older boys off the couch, freeing up space for Candy and Miss Stacey. Candy sat on the edge and left them after a few minutes to see if there was anything to help with in the kitchen. Mostly, she wanted to give their budding friendship some space.

Lyla came in while Candy loaded the dishwasher.

"Oh, you don't have to do that."

"I know, but it gives me something to do."

Lyla helped rinse and hand the dishes to Candy.

"So, Miss Stacey, huh?" Lyla asked.

Candy looked up blushing at the transparency of her plan, "I hope you don't mind."

Giggling, Lyla said, "Mind? Oh, honey, we don't mind.

And if it distracts him from how much we 'neglect' him," she said making air quotes, "then we'll all be sending you a Christmas card next year."

When Candy and Lyla had finished in the kitchen, Candy walked back to the living room.

"Shall we go?" she asked Miss Stacey.

Mr. Lewiston glared at her, but she ignored it, knowing she'd felt the same when Edie took Jace today. Inwardly, she sighed. She missed him already.

Too soon, she returned to her empty house. Leaning against the door, she looked around. It was the same barren place she'd left. Tucked in the branches of her tree was a small box. Her heart pounded. Had someone come in her house while she was away? The silence pressed around her. She shook off the somber mood and retrieved the gift. 'Merry Christmas' had been scrawled across the top. The lid lifted off easily to reveal a key chain in the shape of a nurse's cap. The little red cross sparkled with tiny crystals. A sapphire-blue crystal heart hung from the ring above it. A gift card to the restaurant Hearth lay below the key chain. She looked back at the message. Jace. She hadn't gotten him anything, and all she had done was take him on a wild hike. At least it had been memorable. She touched her hairline, where she'd smacked her head on the tree. It would be tender for a few days.

A knock on the door startled Candy. What she found on the other side surprised her even more. Jace stood waiting, his jacket open and his hands stuffed into his pockets. Panic surrounded her. There was only one reason Jace would be standing on her doorstep. She grabbed his lapels, noting the solid muscles beneath his jacket, but there wasn't time for that.

"What happened to Edie? Where is she? Is she okay?" she

asked, her breath creating a momentary fog between them.

He raised his hands and covered hers, pressing them against his chest Why did that have to spark fire even in the midst of an emergency?

"Grandma is fine. She's at my parents still."

Candy didn't understand.

"But … then why are you here?"

He lifted a shoulder, "Sometimes you choose a direction and God gently nudges you in a better one." He smiled, a flash of mischief in his eyes. "Come for a drive?"

A drive, maybe, but first, she'd regretted all day the mess she'd made of what she'd thought of as her 'second chance' this morning. They said the third time was the charm. It was time to test that theory. She pulled him into the house, kicking the door shut. Before her courage failed, she backed him up against the door and pressed her lips to his. She wanted this man and she didn't care if she had to go back to the city or not. Home was wherever he was. His arms went around her, pulling her flush against him. His warm mouth tasted faintly of mint. She hoped the kiss held promises she couldn't yet speak. His hands went to her hair and he tilted her head back. His breath was shallow and fast, his eyes piercing as if to extract all her darkest secrets. Oh, what had she done? She stepped away.

"Sorry," she said fighting for air. "I'll get my coat."

He stepped toward her. Before she could move, he held her face in both hands. The scared part of her wanted to run, to protect her heart, but something about him drew her in.

"Candy," he said, his tone drenching her in longing.

His phone vibrated, but he ignored it, caressing her lower lip with his thumb. She flicked her tongue around it enjoying the surprise on his face. He tugged her close and smothered her mouth with his. Melting into him, she marveled at how perfect they fit together.

Several minutes later Candy, ducked into Jace's shoulder to catch her breath. Jace stroked her hair.

"While I could stay here all night, kissing you, love," he murmured near her ear. "There is something I want to show you if you're up for it."

Candy nodded and said, "Of course."

Jace helped her with her coat and held her hand all the way to the car. They drove through the festive streets, listening to Christmas songs on the radio. Jace hummed along, sometimes singing. He looked so content and confident. They approached the main square, where several people walked arm-in-arm around the town Christmas tree, but they didn't stop there. A few streets over Jace made a left and parked.

"Wait here," he said.

He jogged around the car and opened the door for her.

"You're sure you have no girlfriend? No wife?"

How could this man not already be taken? It defied reason.

"Earlier I would have said 'No to both', but I'm hoping that's changed," he said slipping his arm around her waist.

She gazed up at him. "I hope so, too," she said smiling. That 'third time's a charm' thing had really worked.

He kissed her until a passing car honked, startling both of them. Laughing, he pointed across the street to a vacant building. Enormous letters spelling 'Le Boulangerie' ran along the roofline. The paint had faded to almost non-existence in some places. Paper, yellowed with age, covered large windows in the front. In a few spots, boards covered broken panes. It obviously hadn't been occupied in some time.

"The old bakery," Jace said. A hint of wistfulness

accompanied the words.

"It looks like it was abandoned a while ago."

She hoped he would tell her about it, about why it meant something to him.

"Yeah. Grandpa Henry opened it when he and Grandma were young. Want to see the inside?" He took her hand and started toward the building.

The lock opened easily. Inside, light from the street lamps glowed through the upper windows, reflecting on the ceiling. The large space had a bit of character from the little she could see. Decorative woodwork ran along the walls and around doors and windows.

"Sorry, I know there isn't much light, but I didn't want to wait until tomorrow." He activated his phone's flashlight but it didn't make much difference.

"The woodwork is lovely," she said, running her finger along a chair rail. "So much detail and history."

"What else do you see?"

She surveyed the area, knowing he saw the same empty room she did. Then it occurred to her that it wasn't what was actually there that he was asking about. Letting her imagination wander she said, "Over in the front corner, a two-storey library, with seating by the windows and open to this front area. Maybe a little cafe, like the bookstore in the city. Possibly some offices in the back." Coming back to him, she asked, "What do you see?"

"Definitely a library in that corner," he said pointing to the space she'd indicated. "And offices back there." He motioned behind them.

"Yes. But who's going to open a library?"

He brought her close again. She couldn't even think. Doing what came naturally, she slid her arms around his waist. Quiet strength and excitement saturated the air near him.

"Not just a library." He stared at her for a moment before continuing, "Long story short, my family owns this building. I complained to my sister that another woman was trying to wreck my career after you were picketing." A bit embarrassed, Candy stepped back. Jace didn't let go of her however. "I realized you weren't there to sabotage the project, that you were thinking about the community." He pulled her close again. "I like when you are close," he murmured into her hair. He took a breath and continued, "I also talked to my dad a little bit about it last week, and then today I discovered that their neighbor is the president of Mack Community College."

"Oh, wow."

"My dad had talked to President Wixom. She and her husband came over to my parents' house this afternoon. Essentially, she and my dad have been working out a deal where the school will buy this building, renovate, and move the satellite campus here."

Candy's hand flew to her chest and she said, "Jace. That's incredible."

"Yes, but even more incredible? She asked if I would work on the project."

A pit formed in Candy's stomach. "But, you don't want to be here."

"Remember the nudge I talked about earlier?"

She nodded.

"I had been so afraid to come back, afraid that people would judge me and that the discontent would destroy me."

Jace tucked a stray hair behind her ear. She couldn't help leaning into his palm. He caressed her cheek as he watched her and after a moment continued.

"When I got here, I found that people accepted me, were

actually friendly. It felt like an extension of my family, the opposite of what I expected. The restlessness I imagined didn't exist. But I did discover something when I went back to the city today." His face grew serious.

"What?"

"That while I was here, distracted by work on a project, a thief crept in and swiped something I'd been protecting quite vigilantly."

Not wanting to jump to conclusions, she asked, "What do you mean? Are you sure?"

He chuckled. "I'm one hundred percent sure. The question is, 'What do you intend to do with my heart now that you've stolen it?'"

Her eyes widened. Searching his face for any trace of deceit, she let what he'd said sink in. Maybe Christmas romances could be a good thing.

"Your heart?" she asked smiling up at him.

"Yes, my heart. What are you going to do with it?"

"I promise to take the best care of it," she whispered. She kissed him tenderly then looked in his eyes. "I love Saint Angelo, but I love you more Jace. And I want to be with you. Wherever you are." Where this courage had come from, she didn't know, but that spark of warmth seemed to have exploded within her.

"I love you too," he said kissing her forehead. "I believe St. A is where I am supposed to end up, but it may require a detour to the city." He explained about the teaching position at the main campus.

She laughed. "Do you mind if I tag along? Because this nursing degree won't earn itself."

"You want to leave St. A?"

"As long as it's temporary." She regarded him, the emotion threatening to overcome her, and she confessed

228

softly, "But really, as long as you're with me, that's all that matters."

He kissed her again with the promise of the future in every breath.

THE END

Reviews

If you liked this story, please consider leaving a review. You can always connect with the author on Facebook, Instagram, her blog, or Twitter as well.

Acknowledgements

There are so many people who contribute along the path of writing a story. To those who've helped, thank you! Inevitably, someone will get left off the list. This is not intentional. But I do want to give a shout out to the major players: the Wednesday warriors: Anika Arrington, Tamara Passey, and Valerie Ipson; my sisters: Mindy, Jodi, Diana, and Mom; technical knowledge go-to people: Susan Geer, Zach Banta, and John Richards; my editor: Kathryn Olsen; and not least, my husband and kids who've put up with the craziness that comes with deadlines.

About the Author

Peggy Urry is a small town girl who loves the city and the ocean (and the mountains as long as she doesn't have to camp or hike). She credits the lack of television in her parents' home for her love of reading and her imagination. She credits the guy who's been hanging the moon for over 25 years for her belief in romance and true love. Five wonderful children, extended family, and great friends keep life exciting.

Find a book you love and read!

Made in the USA
San Bernardino, CA
20 November 2018